P9-CEL-420

READ-ALOUD RHYMES FOR THE VERY YOUNG

READ-ALOUD RHYMES

FOR THE VERY YOUNG

SELECTED BY
JACK PRELUTSKY

ILLUSTRATED BY
MARC BROWN

With an Introduction by
JIM TRELEASE

DRAGONFLY BOOKS NEW YORK

Text copyright © 1986 by Alfred A. Knopf
Jacket art and interior illustrations copyright © 1986 by Marc Brown
Introduction copyright © 1986 by Jim Trelease

All rights reserved. Published in the United States by Dragonfly Books, an imprint of Random House Children's Books, a division of Penguin Random House LLC, New York. Originally published in hardcover in the United States by Alfred A. Knopf, an imprint of Random House Children's Books, New York, in 1986.

Dragonfly Books with the colophon is a registered trademark of Penguin Random House LLC.

Visit us on the Web! randomhousekids.com

Educators and librarians, for a variety of teaching tools, visit us at RHTeachersLibrarians.com

The Library of Congress has cataloged the hardcover edition of this work as follows:
Read-aloud rhymes for the very young / selected by Jack Prelutsky ;
illustrated by Marc Brown ; with an introduction by Jim Trelease.
Summary: A collection of more than 200 short poems by both known
and anonymous American and English authors.
ISBN 978-0-394-87218-6 (trade) — ISBN 978-0-394-97218-3 (lib. bdg.) — ISBN 978-0-399-55357-8 (pbk.)
1. Children's poetry, American. 2. Children's poetry, English. 3. Nursery rhymes.
[1. American poetry—Collections. 2. English poetry—Collections.]
I. Prelutsky, Jack. II. Brown, Marc Tolon, ill.
PS586.3.R4 1986 811'.008'09282 86007147

MANUFACTURED IN CHINA
10 9 8 7 6 5 4 3 2 1
First Dragonfly Books Edition

Random House Children's Books supports the First Amendment and celebrates the right to read.

For Janet Schulman

–J.P.

Drawn with love for Eliza Morgan Brown

–M.B.

INTRODUCTION

EVERYONE is aware that children are great *asking machines*. Indeed, research shows us that children ask about thirty questions an hour: Who? What? When? Where? Why? And with good reason, for these questions are the principal tools children use to discover and understand the world around them.

However, most adults forget that long before children become great asking machines, they are great *listening machines*. The newborn infant is a marvelously discerning listener, always reacting to a woman's voice instead of a man's when both speak simultaneously. And why not? He's been listening almost exclusively to the frequency of a woman's voice for the last nine months. Within ten weeks after birth this acuity has grown to the point where the average baby can pick out his mother's voice from all others. Pretty sharp listener for such a little person, wouldn't you say?

The relevance of all this to a collection of poetry is demonstrated by the fact that the first sound a child hears is actually a poem—the rhythmic, rhyming beat-beat-beat of a mother's heart. This early and fundamental relationship sets the stage for a natural and lifelong love of rhythm and rhyme. It's demonstrated by the ease with which young children learn anything set to music, such as TV commercials, the way they are lulled to sleep by the repetitious purr of a motor, and their tendency to sing or hum songs when they are happy. And songs are, after all, nothing more than poetry set to music.

No one better recognizes the essence of the child-poetry connection than poet and anthologist Jack Prelutsky. What he accomplished for older children in *The Random House Book of Poetry*, he has duplicated for younger children in *Read-Aloud Rhymes for the Very Young*. Here are more than two hundred little poems to feed little people with little attention spans to help both grow. Marc Brown's inviting illustrations add a visual dimension to the poems, which further engage young imaginations.

Children have a near-genius capacity to absorb and process language between twelve months and six years of age, learning an average of nine new words a day. Research further shows us that the richer and more plentiful the language environment, the richer will be the child's vocabulary. The child will learn to read more easily, and will have fewer learning difficulties. Simply put, if the child has never *heard* the word, the child will never *say* the word; and if you have neither heard it nor said it, it's pretty tough to *read* it and to *write* it.

Next to hugging and talking to children, reading aloud is the greatest gift we can give them. Beyond the positive role modeling and physical bonding taking place, we are stimulating imagination, enriching vocabulary, building listening skills, and whetting the appetite for a love of reading.

Over the years we have discovered a pattern in *which* words children learn. They choose first those words with some personal meaning—Mommy, Daddy, Nana, milk, cup, potty, dog, water, shoe, etc. This pattern continues right into adult life. The poets included in this collection know this instinctively. They use words that relate to what children see and feel every day. So you'll find words here about bedtime, moon and stars, about mornings, noses, and sneezes. They know little people are naturally interested by little things: mittens, butterflies, chicks, crumbs, snowflakes, kittens, mice, caterpillars, and ants. And thus they populate their poetry with them. They also know that children's imaginations gravitate to nonsense and wonder, music and thunder; therefore they also write about elves and fairies, shadows and dragons. As the vocabulary grows, so too does comprehension and attention span.

"Read it again!" is a child's version of "Bravo! Encore, maestro!" The brevity of these poems allows the reader to be generous with encores.

The poets represented in this volume have not forgotten what it was like to be three years old. Frances Frost's poem "Squirrel in the Rain" magically transported me back thirty-five years to an apartment house window where I spent many winter hours pondering the fate and living quarters of tiny gray squirrels across the street. Reading such poems aloud allows us to visit with the child within each of us, and each visit gives us a better understanding of the child on our lap or in our classroom.

Unlike the toys we buy our children, poems cannot break. Their flavor will last longer than a hundred boxes of candy. They come already assembled and need only one battery—a reader connected to one child. And that reader can start a glow that lasts a lifetime.

JIM TRELEASE
Springfield, Massachusetts
May 1986

SINGING-TIME

I wake in the morning early
And always, the very first thing,
I poke out my head and I sit up in bed
And I sing and I sing and I sing.

Rose Fyleman

The Raggedy Dog

The Raggedy Dog chased the Raggedy Cat
And she climbed to the top of a tree;
So the Raggedy Dog came a-running and sat
Underneath until quarter-past three.

That night as the moon rose over the hill
And the Raggedy Man came around,
The Cat lay asleep in the branches so still,
And the Dog was asleep on the ground.

Sherman Ripley

The Snail and the Mouse

The Snail and the Mouse
Went round the house,
Running a race together;
The riders were elves,
And proud of themselves,
For neither weighed more than a feather.

The Snail went crawly, creepy, crawl,
The Mouse went hoppety hop, sir;
But they came to a fence
That *was* so immense
(Six inches!), they *had* to stop, sir!

Laura E. Richards

A Frog and a Flea

A frog and a flea
And a kangaroo
Once jumped for a prize
In a pot of glue;
The kangaroo stuck
And so did the flea,
And the frog limped home
With a fractured knee.

Cynthia Mitchell

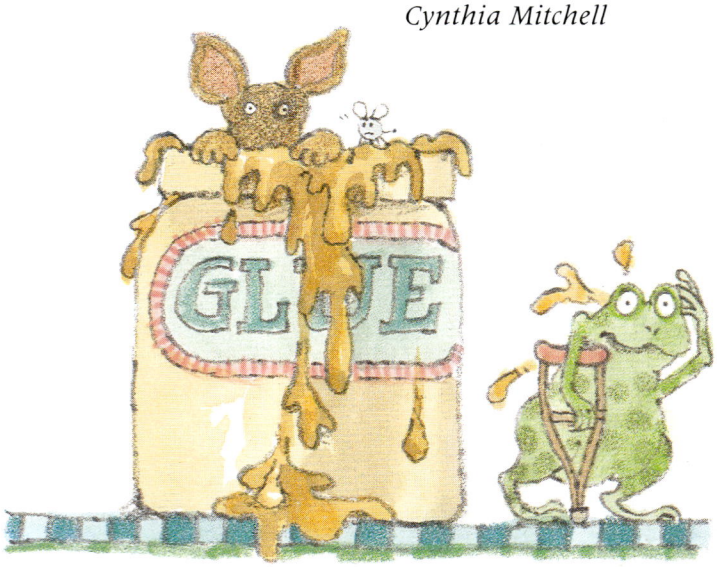

Higglety, Pigglety, Pop!

Higglety, pigglety, pop!
The dog has eaten the mop;
  The pig's in a hurry,
  The cat's in a flurry,
Higglety, pigglety, pop!

Samuel Goodrich

Run a Little

Run a little this way,
  Run a little that!
Fine new feathers
  For a fine new hat.
A fine new hat
  For a lady fair–
Run round and turn about
  And jump in the air.

Run a little this way,
  Run a little that!
White silk ribbon
  For a black silk cat.
A black silk cat
  For the Lord Mayor's wife–
Run around and turn about
  And fly for your life!

James Reeves

Just Watch

Watch
how high
I'm jumping,

Watch
how far
I hop,

Watch
how long
I'm skipping,

Watch
how fast
I stop!

Myra Cohn Livingston

Whistling

Oh, I can laugh and I can sing
and I can scream and shout,
but when I try to whistle,
the whistle won't come out.

I shape my lips the proper way,
I make them small and round,
but when I blow, just air comes out,
there is no whistling sound.

But I'll keep trying very hard
to whistle loud and clear,
and someday soon I'll whistle tunes
for everyone to hear.

Jack Prelutsky

Jump or Jiggle

Frogs jump
Caterpillars hump

Worms wiggle
Bugs jiggle

Rabbits hop
Horses clop

Snakes slide
Sea gulls glide

Mice creep
Deer leap

Puppies bounce
Kittens pounce

Lions stalk–
But–
I walk!

Evelyn Beyer

Hide and Seek

When I am alone, and quite alone,
I play a game, and it's all my own.

I hide myself
Behind myself,
And then I try
To find myself.

I hide in the closet,
Where no one can see;
Then I start looking
Around for me.

I hide myself
And look for myself;
There once was a shadow
I took for myself.

I hide in a corner;
I hide in the bed;
And when I come near me
I pull in my head!

A. B. Shiffrin

Footnote

Isn't it foolish to dash off outside
Before making sure that your shoelace is tied?
How silly you'll look when you trip in the street
And land on your fanny instead of your feet!

Norah Smaridge

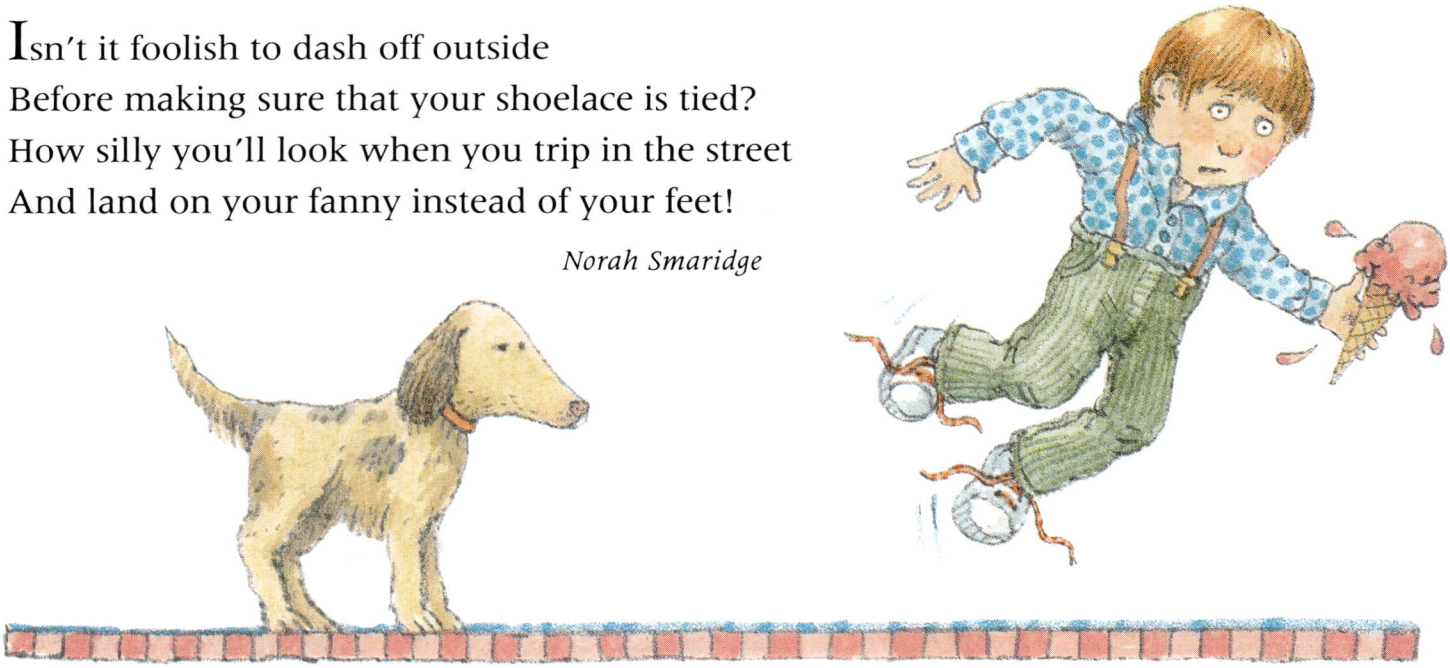

Swimming

Watch me swim!
I lie down so

And make my hands
And both feet go;

I blow to keep
The water away;

And breathe with ease
In the proper way.

I can swim fine
As fine can be

So long as I
Keep out of the sea.

Alice Higgins

Dangerous

When we're
Hunting
We explore
Squares upon the
kitchen floor;
We must
Get from
Here to there
Without touching
Anywhere;
For this
Square is
Safe for us.
But that one is
Dangerous.

Dorothy Aldis

Blowing Bubbles

Dip your pipe and gently blow.
Watch the tiny bubble grow
Big and bigger, round and fat,
Rainbow-colored, and then—
SPLAT!

Margaret Hillert

An Old Person of Ware

There was an old person of Ware,
Who rode on the back of a bear:
When they asked, "Does it trot?"
He said, "Certainly not!
He's a Moppsikon Floppsikon bear!"

Edward Lear

Polar Bear

The secret of the polar bear
Is that he wears long underwear.

Gail Kredenser

The Elephant Carries a Great Big Trunk

The elephant carries a great big trunk;
He never packs it with clothes;
It has no lock and it has no key,
But he takes it wherever he goes.

Anonymous

Holding Hands

Elephants walking
Along the trails

Are holding hands
By holding tails

Trunks and tails
Are handy things

When elephants walk
In circus rings.

Elephants work
And elephants play

And elephants walk
And feel so gay.

And when they walk–
It never fails

They're holding hands
By holding tails.

Lenore M. Link

Showers

Squelch and squirt and squiggle,
Drizzle and drip and drain–
Such a lot of water
Comes down with the rain!

Marchette Chute

Little Wind

Little wind, blow on the hill-top,
  Little wind, blow down the plain;
Little wind, blow up the sunshine,
  Little wind, blow off the rain.

Kate Greenaway

The Rain

Rain on the green grass,
  And rain on the tree,
And rain on the housetop,
  But not upon me!

Anonymous

Rainy Day

I do not like a rainy day.
The road is wet, the sky is gray.
They dress me up, from head to toes,
In lots and lots of rubber clothes.
I wish the sun would come and stay.
I do not like a rainy day.

William Wise

Mud

Mud is very nice to feel
All squishy-squash between the toes!
I'd rather wade in wiggly mud
Than smell a yellow rose.

Nobody else but the rosebush knows
How nice mud feels
Between the toes.

Polly Chase Boyden

Sun After Rain

Rain, rain,
went away.
Sun came out
with pipe of clay,
blew a bubble
whole-world-wide,
stuck a rainbow
on one side.

Norma Farber

A Spike of Green

When I went out
The sun was hot,
It shone upon
My flower pot.

And there I saw
A spike of green
That no one else
Had ever seen!

On other days
The things I see
Are mostly old
Except for me.

But this green spike
So new and small
Had never yet
Been seen at all!

Barbara Baker

Little Seeds

Little seeds we sow in spring,
growing while the robins sing,
give us carrots, peas and beans,
tomatoes, pumpkins, squash and greens.

And we pick them,
one and all,
through the summer,
through the fall.

Winter comes, then spring, and then
little seeds we sow again.

Else Holmelund Minarik

Halfway Down

Halfway down the stairs
Is a stair
Where I sit.
There isn't any
Other stair
Quite like
It.
I'm not at the bottom,
I'm not at the top;
So this is the stair
Where
I always
Stop.

Halfway up the stairs
Isn't up,
And isn't down.
It isn't in the nursery,
It isn't in the town.
And all sorts of funny thoughts
Run round my head:
"It isn't really
Anywhere!
It's somewhere else
Instead!"

A. A. Milne

Wild Beasts

I will be a lion
  And you shall be a bear,
And each of us will have a den
  Beneath a nursery chair;
And you must growl and growl and growl,
  And I will roar and roar,
And then—why, then—you'll growl again,
  And I will roar some more!

Evaleen Stein

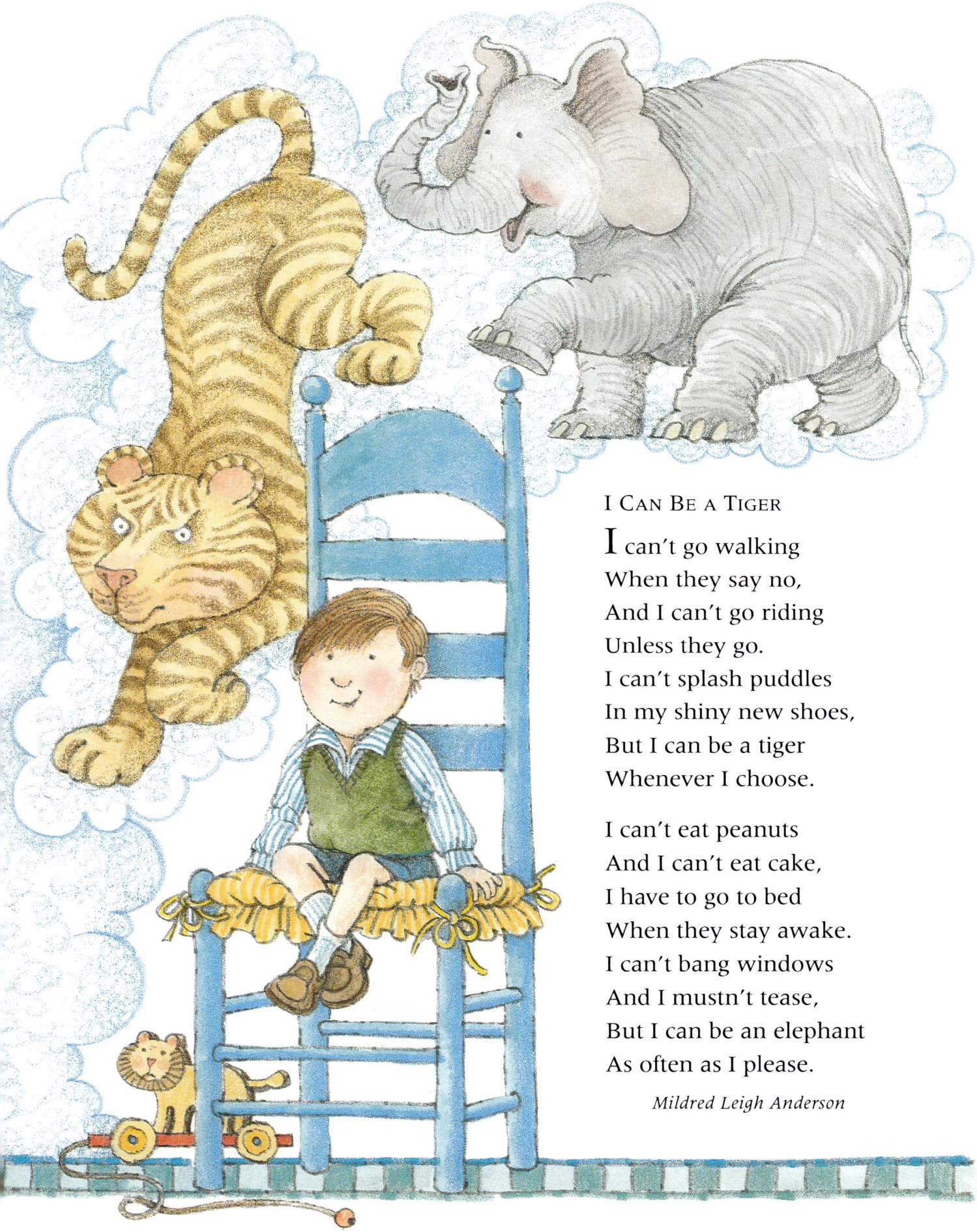

I Can Be a Tiger

I can't go walking
When they say no,
And I can't go riding
Unless they go.
I can't splash puddles
In my shiny new shoes,
But I can be a tiger
Whenever I choose.

I can't eat peanuts
And I can't eat cake,
I have to go to bed
When they stay awake.
I can't bang windows
And I mustn't tease,
But I can be an elephant
As often as I please.

Mildred Leigh Anderson

The House Cat

The house cat sits
And smiles and sings.
He knows a lot
Of secret things.

Annette Wynne

Cat Kisses

Sandpaper kisses
on a cheek or a chin–
that is the way
for a day to begin!

Sandpaper kisses–
a cuddle, a purr.
I have an alarm clock
that's covered with fur.

Bobbi Katz

At Night

When night is dark
my cat is wise
to light the lanterns
in his eyes.

Aileen Fisher

Mother Cat's Purr

Sleep the half-sleep,
Kittens dear,
While your mother
Cat-naps near.

Every kitten
Is a cat,
And you must
Remember that

Naps for cats
Are mostly fake:
Any time
Is time to wake,

Or time to pounce,
Or time to scat.
That's what sleep is—
For a cat.

Jane Yolen

The Little Turtle

There was a little turtle.
He lived in a box.
He swam in a puddle.
He climbed on the rocks.

He snapped at a mosquito.
He snapped at a flea.
He snapped at a minnow.
And he snapped at me.

He caught the mosquito.
He caught the flea.
He caught the minnow.
But he didn't catch me.

Vachel Lindsay

A Big Turtle

A big turtle sat on the end of a log,
Watching a tadpole turn into a frog.

Anonymous

Snail's Pace

Maybe it's so
that snails are slow.
They trudge along and tarry.

But isn't it true
you'd slow up, too,
if you had a house to carry?

Aileen Fisher

The Toad

I met a little woman
who was going up a hill,
and when she wasn't hopping,
she sat extremely still.

She hadn't any neck at all,
she hadn't any chin,
she opened wide her great big mouth
and snapped a young fly in.

She seemed to be good-natured,
and friendly as could be,
for while she swallowed down the fly,
she winked her eye at me.

Elizabeth Coatsworth

The Frog on the Log

There once
Was a green
  Little frog, frog, frog–

Who played
In the wood
  On a log, log, log!

A screech owl
Sitting
  In a tree, tree, tree–

Came after
The frog
  With a scree, scree, scree!

When the frog
Heard the owl–
  In a flash, flash, flash–

He leaped
In the pond
  With a splash, splash, splash!

Ilo Orleans

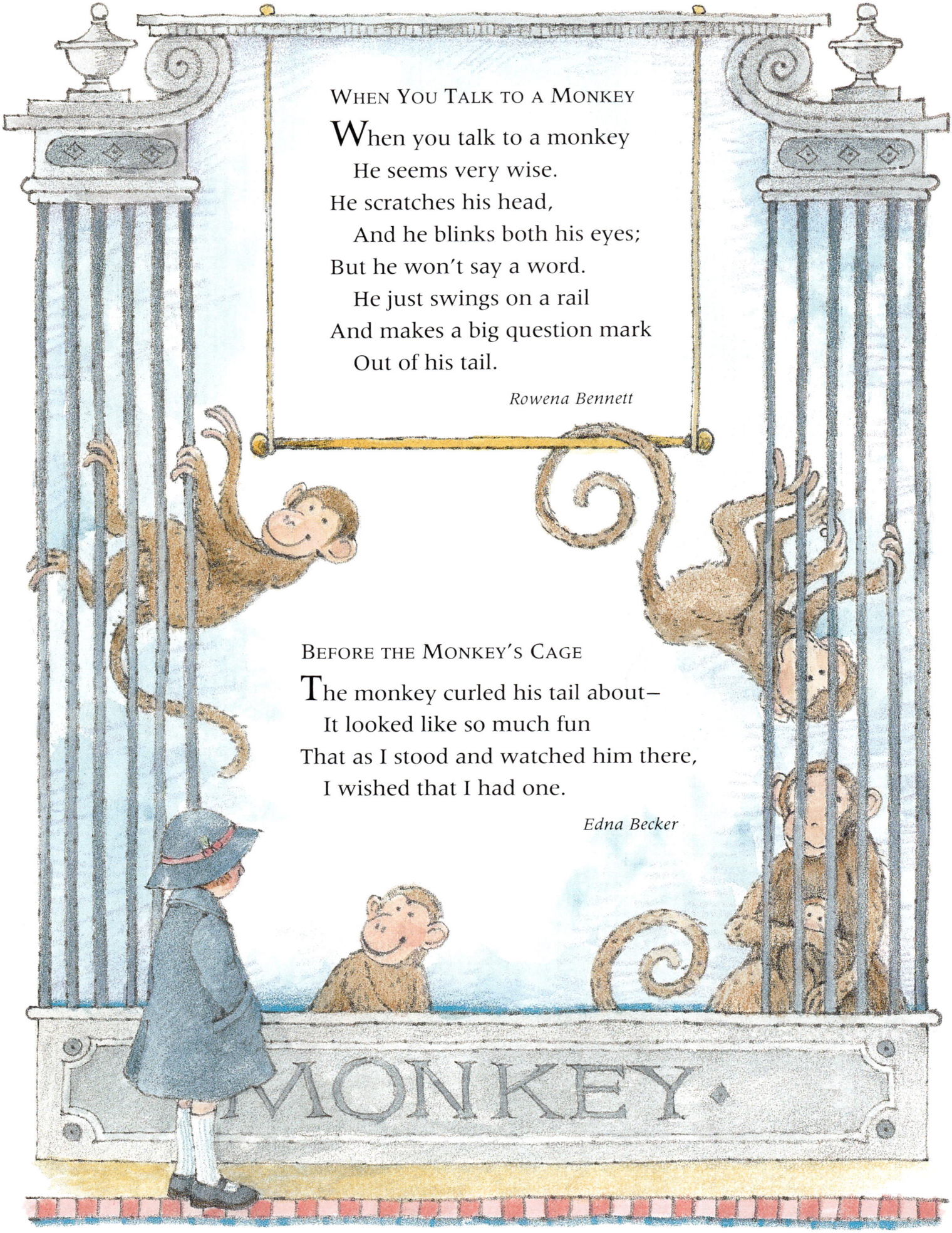

When You Talk to a Monkey

When you talk to a monkey
  He seems very wise.
He scratches his head,
  And he blinks both his eyes;
But he won't say a word.
  He just swings on a rail
And makes a big question mark
  Out of his tail.

Rowena Bennett

Before the Monkey's Cage

The monkey curled his tail about–
  It looked like so much fun
That as I stood and watched him there,
  I wished that I had one.

Edna Becker

Humming Birds

I think it is a funny thing
That some birds whistle, others sing.
The Warbler warbles in his throat,
The Sparrow only knows one note;
But he is better off than some,
For Humming Birds can only hum.

Betty Sage

Singing in the Spring

As I was walking along-long-long,
singing a scrap of a song-song-song,
a Blackbird perched in a tree-tree-tree
he whistled my song with me-me-me;
he whistled so sweet and high-high-high
his notes tangled up with the sky-sky-sky!

Ivy O. Eastwick

The Swallow

Swallow, swallow, swooping free,
Do you not remember me?
I think last spring that it was you
Who tumbled down the sooty flue
With wobbly wings and gaping face,
A fledgling in the fireplace.

Remember how I nursed and fed you,
And then into the air I sped you?
How I wish that you would try
To take me with you as you fly.

Ogden Nash

Woodpecker in Disguise

Woodpecker taps at the apple tree.
"Little bug, open your door," says he.
Little bug says, "Who is it, sir?"
Woodpecker says, "The carpenter."

Grace Taber Hallock

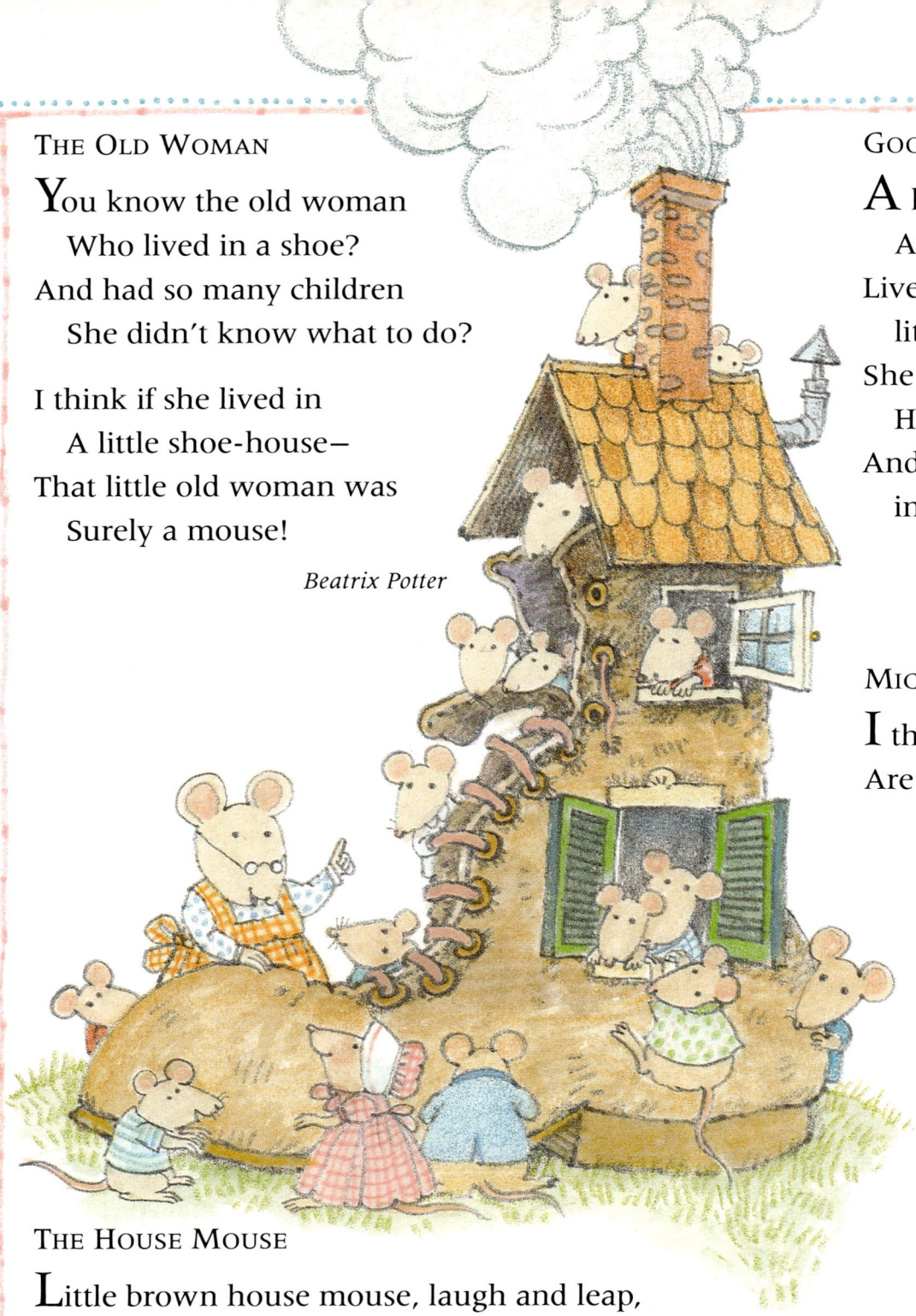

The Old Woman

You know the old woman
  Who lived in a shoe?
And had so many children
  She didn't know what to do?

I think if she lived in
  A little shoe-house–
That little old woman was
  Surely a mouse!

Beatrix Potter

Good Neighbors

A little old woman
  And a little old mouse
Live in the very same
  little old house.
She rocks in a corner,
  He scampers in the wall,
And they never, never get
  in each other's way at all.

May Justus

Mice

I think mice
Are rather nice.

Their tails are long,
Their faces small,
They haven't any
Chins at all.
Their ears are pink,
Their teeth are white,
They run about
The house at night.
They nibble things
They shouldn't touch
And no one seems
To like them much.

But *I* think mice
Are nice.

Rose Fyleman

The House Mouse

Little brown house mouse, laugh and leap,
chitter and cheep while the cat's asleep,
chatter and call and slip through the wall,
trip through the kitchen, skip through the hall.

Little brown house mouse, don't be meek,
dance and squeak and prance and tweak.
There's cheese to take and plenty of cake
as long as you're gone when the cat's awake.

Jack Prelutsky

Hide-and-Seek Shadow

I walked with my shadow,
I ran with my shadow,
I danced with my shadow,
I did.
Then a cloud came over
And the sun went under
And my shadow stopped playing
And hid.

Margaret Hillert

Poor Shadow

Everything has a shadow–
A mountain, a bird or a ball–
Only a poor, poor shadow
Hasn't a shadow at all!

Ilo Orleans

Look

Firelight and shadows
dancing on the wall.
Look at my shadow
TEN FEET TALL!

Charlotte Zolotow

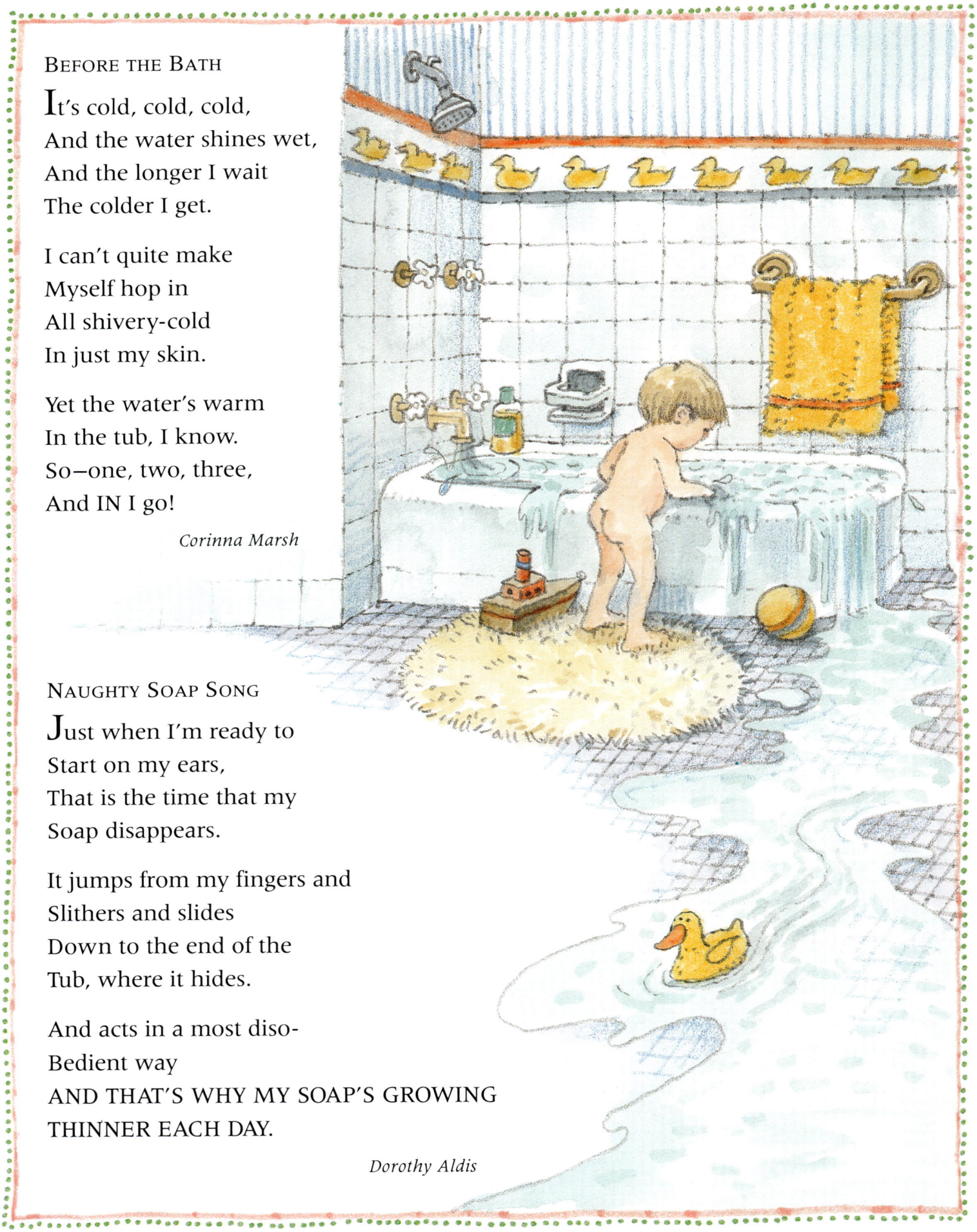

Before the Bath

It's cold, cold, cold,
And the water shines wet,
And the longer I wait
The colder I get.

I can't quite make
Myself hop in
All shivery-cold
In just my skin.

Yet the water's warm
In the tub, I know.
So—one, two, three,
And IN I go!

Corinna Marsh

Naughty Soap Song

Just when I'm ready to
Start on my ears,
That is the time that my
Soap disappears.

It jumps from my fingers and
Slithers and slides
Down to the end of the
Tub, where it hides.

And acts in a most diso-
Bedient way
AND THAT'S WHY MY SOAP'S GROWING
THINNER EACH DAY.

Dorothy Aldis

The Way They Scrub

The way they scrub
Me in the tub,
I think there's
Hardly
Any
Doubt
Sometime they'll rub
And rub and rub
Until they simply
Rub
Me
Out.

A. B. Ross

Wish

If I could wish,
I'd be a fish
(For just a day or two)
To flip and flash
And dart and splash
And nothing else to do,
And never anyone to say,
"Are you quite sure you washed today?"
I'd like it, wouldn't you?

Dorothy Brown Thompson

Happy Winter, Steamy Tub

Happy Winter, steamy tub
To soak and splash in, wash and rub.
Big blobs of bubbles pile on me
The way the snow sits on a tree.
I rinse the soap off, scrub some more,
Drip puddles on the bathroom floor–
Then gurgling bubbles drain away,
A wet and merry end of day.

Karen Gundersheimer

Big

Now I can catch and throw a ball
And spell
Cat. Dog.
And Pig,
I have finished being small
And started
Being Big.

Dorothy Aldis

Something About Me

There's something about me
That I'm knowing.
There's something about me
That isn't showing.

I'm growing!

Anonymous

The World

The world is big,
And I am small.
The houses all
Are wide and tall.
I run and turn
And trip and fall!

I am so small!
I come and go.
I cannot see,
I cannot know.
I hope it won't
Be always so.

Barbara Young

My Sister Laura

My sister Laura's bigger than me
And lifts me up quite easily.
I can't lift her, I've tried and tried;
She must have something heavy inside.

Spike Milligan

Five Years Old

Please, everybody, look at me!
Today I'm *five* years old, you see!
And after this, I won't be four,
Not ever, ever, anymore!
I won't be three—or two—or one,
For that was when I'd first begun.
Now I'll be five a while, and then
I'll soon be something else again!

Marie Louise Allen

The Wish

Each birthday wish
I've ever made
Really does come true.
Each year I wish
I'll grow some more
And every year
I
DO!

Ann Friday

Birthdays

If birthdays happened once a week
Instead of once a year,
Think of all the gifts you'd get
And all the songs you'd hear
And think how quickly you'd grow up;
Wouldn't it feel queer
If birthdays happened once a week
Instead of once a year?

Mary Ann Hoberman

Baby's Baking

So, so, spade and hoe,
  Little pile of sand;
See it turning into dough
  In the baby's hand!

Little pie with crimpy crust,
  Set it in the sun;
Sugar it with powdered dust,
  And bake it till it's done.

Evaleen Stein

Home

The sea is ringed around with hills
And scalloped with white foam;
I've filled my pockets full of shells
And now I'm going home.

Jean Jaszi

Shore

Play on the seashore
And gather up shells,
Kneel in the damp sands
Digging wells.

Run on the rocks
Where the seaweed slips,
Watch the waves
And the beautiful ships.

Mary Britton Miller

We Built a Castle Near the Rocks

We built a castle near the rocks,
we built it out of sand.

Our fortress was an ice-cream box
with turret, tall and grand.

Our men were twigs, our guns were straws
from which we'd sipped at lunch.

We had the very best of wars . . .
till someone's foot
went
CRUNCH!

Joan Walsh Anglund

The Picnic

We brought a rug for sitting on,
Our lunch was in a box.
The sand was warm. We didn't wear
Hats or shoes or socks.

Waves came curling up the beach.
We waded. It was fun.
Our sandwiches were different kinds.
I dropped my jelly one.

Dorothy Aldis

Picnic Day

Sing a song of picnics,
  Bread and butter spread,
Greenery all around about,
  And cherries overhead!

Rachel Field

Joyful

A summer day is full of ease,
a bank is full of money,
our lilac bush is full of bees,
and I am full of honey.

Rose Burgunder

August Heat

In August, when the days are hot,
I like to find a shady spot,
And hardly move a single bit–
And sit–
  And sit–
    And sit–
      And sit!

Anonymous

WOULDN'T YOU?

If I
Could go
As high
And low
As the wind
As the wind
As the wind
Can blow–

I'd go!

John Ciardi

A KITE

I often sit and wish that I
Could be a kite up in the sky,
And ride upon the breeze and go
Whichever way I chanced to blow.

Anonymous

THE BUTTERFLY

Up and down the air you float
Like a little fairy boat;
I should like to sail the sky,
Gliding like a butterfly!

Clinton Scollard

THE GOLD-TINTED DRAGON

What's the good of a wagon
Without any dragon
To pull you for mile after mile?
An elegant lean one
A gold-tinted green one
Wearing a dragonly smile.
You'll sweep down the valleys
You'll sail up the hills
Your dragon will shine in the sun
And as you rush by
The people will cry
"I wish that my wagon had one!"

Karla Kuskin

The Toaster

A silver-scaled Dragon with jaws flaming red
Sits at my elbow and toasts my bread.
I hand him fat slices, and then, one by one,
He hands them back when he sees they are done.

William Jay Smith

My Dragon

I have a purple dragon
With a long brass tail that clangs,
And anyone not nice to me
Soon feels his fiery fangs,

So if you tell me I'm a dope
Or call my muscles jelly,
You just might dwell a billion years
Inside his boiling belly.

X. J. Kennedy

A Modern Dragon

A train is a dragon that roars through the dark.
He wriggles his tail as he sends up a spark.
He pierces the night with his one yellow eye,
And all the earth trembles when he rushes by.

Rowena Bennett

The Pigs

Piggie Wig and Piggie Wee,
Hungry pigs as pigs could be,
For their dinner had to wait
Down behind the barnyard gate.

Piggie Wig and Piggie Wee
Climbed the barnyard gate to see,
Peeping through the gate so high,
But no dinner could they spy.

Piggie Wig and Piggie Wee
Got down sad as pigs could be;
But the gate soon opened wide
And they scampered forth outside.

Piggie Wig and Piggie Wee,
What was their delight to see?
Dinner ready not far off–
Such a full and tempting trough!

Piggie Wig and Piggie Wee,
Greedy pigs as pigs could be,
For their dinner ran pell-mell;
In the trough both piggies fell.

Emilie Poulsson

Mary Middling

Mary Middling had a pig,
Not very little and not very big,
Not very pink, not very green,
Not very dirty, not very clean,
Not very good, not very naughty,
Not very humble, not very haughty,
Not very thin, not very fat;
Now what would you give for a pig like that?

Rose Fyleman

There Was a Small Pig Who Wept Tears

There was a small pig who wept tears
When his mother said, "I'll wash your ears."
As she poured on the soap,
He cried, "Oh, how I hope
This won't happen again for ten years!"

Arnold Lobel

Ten to One

Ten tired tortoises
lying in the sun;
nine nice neighbors
helping everyone;
eight hasty hostesses
preparing toast for tea;
seven salty sailormen
sailing on the sea;
six savage sharks
all swimming through the deep;
five fluttering fireflies
where the moonbeams peep;
four fat foresters
chopping fine fir trees;
three thin thatchers
a'thatching in the breeze;
two tall tailors
sewing at a seam;
and one wild warrior,
very wild warrior,
bow-and-arrow warrior,
eating pink ice-cream.

Ivy O. Eastwick

The Top and the Tip

Hair is the top of a person,
a chimney's the top of a house,
a cover's the top of a book,
the tail is the tip of a mouse.

The sky is the top of the world,
the top of the sky is space,
a flower's the top of the stem,
the nose is the tip of the face.

Charlotte Zolotow

The Very Nicest Place

The fish lives in the brook,
The bird lives in the tree,
But home's the very nicest place
For a little child like me.

Anonymous

Wings

Bees have four wings,
birds have two,
I haven't *any*
and that's too few.

Aileen Fisher

Makers

Beetlebombs make jelly jam
And bumblebees make honey
Mommy makes the bread and cakes
And Easter eggs make bunnies

Bubbling springs make brooks and things
And rivers make the sea
Grownup frogs make pollywogs
But who made me?

Nancy Dingman Watson

Happy Thought

The world is so full of a number of things,
I'm sure we should all be as happy as kings.

Robert Louis Stevenson

The Puppy Chased the Sunbeam

The puppy chased the sunbeam
all around the house–
he thought it was a bee,
or a little golden mouse;
he thought it was a spider
on a little silver string;
he thought it was a butterfly
or some such flying thing;
he thought–but oh! I cannot tell you
half the things he thought
as he chased the sparkling sunbeam
which–just–would–not–be–caught.

Ivy O. Eastwick

How a Puppy Grows

I think it's very funny
The way a puppy grows–
A little on his wiggle-tail,
A little on his nose,
A little on his tummy
And a little on his ears;
I guess he'll be a dog all
right
In half a dozen years.

Leroy F. Jackson

Chums

He sits and begs; he gives a paw;
He is, as you can see,
The finest dog you ever saw,
And he belongs to me.

He follows everywhere I go
And even when I swim.
I laugh because he thinks, you know,
That I belong to him.

Arthur Guiterman

SKYSCRAPER

Skyscraper, skyscraper,
Scrape me some sky:
Tickle the sun
While the stars go by.

Tickle the stars
While the sun's climbing high,
Then skyscraper, skyscraper
Scrape me some sky.

Dennis Lee

Chook, Chook

Chook, chook, chook, chook, chook,
Good morning, Mrs. Hen.
How many chickens have you got?
Madam, I've got ten.
Four of them are yellow,
And four of them are brown,
And two of them are speckled red,
The nicest in the town.

Anonymous

Five Little Chickens

Said the first little chicken,
With a queer little squirm,
"I wish I could find
A fat little worm."

Said the next little chicken,
With an odd little shrug,
"I wish I could find
A fat little slug."

Said the third little chicken,
With a sharp little squeal,
"I wish I could find
Some nice yellow meal."

Said the fourth little chicken,
With a small sigh of grief,
"I wish I could find
A little green leaf."

Said the fifth little chicken,
With a faint little moan,
"I wish I could find
A wee gravel stone."

"Now, see here," said the mother,
From the green garden patch,
"If you want your breakfast,
Just come here and scratch."

Anonymous

Quack, Quack!

We have two ducks. One blue. One black.
And when our blue duck goes "Quack-quack"
our black duck quickly quack-quacks back.
The quacks Blue quacks make her quite a quacker
but Black is a quicker quacker-backer.

Dr. Seuss

A Little Talk

The big brown hen and Mrs. Duck
Went walking out together;
They talked about all sorts of things–
The farmyard, and the weather.
But all *I* heard was:
"Cluck! Cluck! Cluck!"
And "Quack! Quack! Quack!"
from Mrs. Duck.

Anonymous

Ducks in the Rain

Ducks are dabbling in the rain,
Dibbling, dabbling in the rain.
Drops of water from each back
Scatter as ducks flap and quack.

I can only stand and look
From my window at the brook,
For I cannot flap and quack
And scatter raindrops from my back.

James S. Tippett

Fish

The little fish are silent
As they swim round and round.
Their mouths are ever talking
A speech without a sound.

Now aren't the fishes funny
To swim in water clear
And talk with words so silent
That nobody can hear?

Arthur S. Bourinot

Fish

Look at them flit
Lickety-split
Wiggling
Swiggling
Swerving
Curving
Hurrying
Scurrying
Chasing
Racing
Whizzing
Whisking
Flying
Frisking
Tearing around
With a leap and a bound
But none of them making the tiniest
tiniest
tiniest
tiniest
sound.

Mary Ann Hoberman

Belly & Tubs Went Out in a Boat

Belly & Tubs went out in a boat,
Tubs wore knickers & Belly a coat,
They got in a quarrel & started to shout
And the boat tipped over & they tumbled out.

Clyde Watson

The Dreadful Doings of Jelly Belly

Jelly Belly bit
  With a big fat bite.
Jelly Belly fought
  With a big fat fight.

Jelly Belly scowled
  With a big fat frown.
Jelly Belly yelled
  Till his house fell down.

Dennis Lee

Slippery Sam

Slippery Sam
Bought a broom,
Ate an apple
And went to the moon;
Swept it clean,
Painted it red,
Came back to earth
And went to bed.

Arnold Spilka

The Huntsmen

Three jolly gentlemen,
  In coats of red,
Rode their horses
  Up to bed.

Three jolly gentlemen
  Snored till morn,
Their horses champing
  The golden corn.

Three jolly gentlemen,
  At break of day,
Came clitter-clatter down the stairs
  And galloped away.

Walter de la Mare

Twinkle, Twinkle

Twinkle, twinkle, little bat!
How I wonder what you're at!
Up above the world you fly,
Like a tea-tray in the sky.
Twinkle, twinkle–

Lewis Carroll

The Donkey

I had a Donkey, that was all right,
But he always wanted to fly my Kite;
Every time I let him, the String would bust.
Your Donkey is better behaved, I trust.

Theodore Roethke

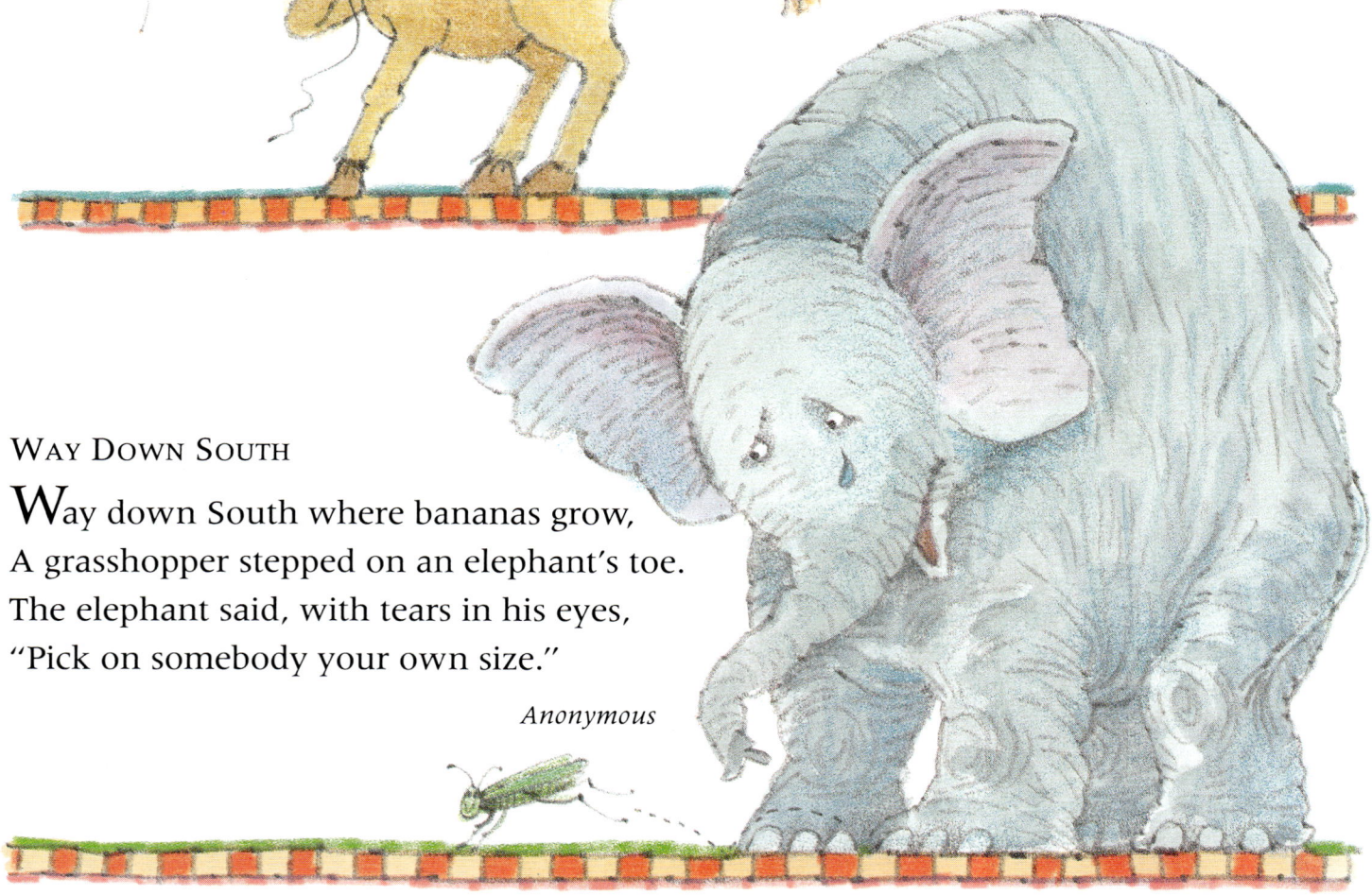

Way Down South

Way down South where bananas grow,
A grasshopper stepped on an elephant's toe.
The elephant said, with tears in his eyes,
"Pick on somebody your own size."

Anonymous

There's Music in a Hammer

There's music in a hammer,
There's music in a nail,
There's music in a pussy cat,
When you step upon her tail.

Anonymous

Fun

I love to hear a lobster
laugh,
Or see a turtle wiggle,
Or poke a hippopotamus
And see the monster giggle,
Or even stand around at
night
And watch the mountains
wriggle.

Leroy F. Jackson

The Toad and the Rabbit

Said the Rabbit to the Hop Toad:
"It's very strange to me
How very big and long and wide
A Hop Toad's *mouth* can be."

Said the Hop Toad to the Rabbit:
"I'm sure I'd shed some tears
If on my head I had to wear
Such flippy-floppy *ears*."

John Martin

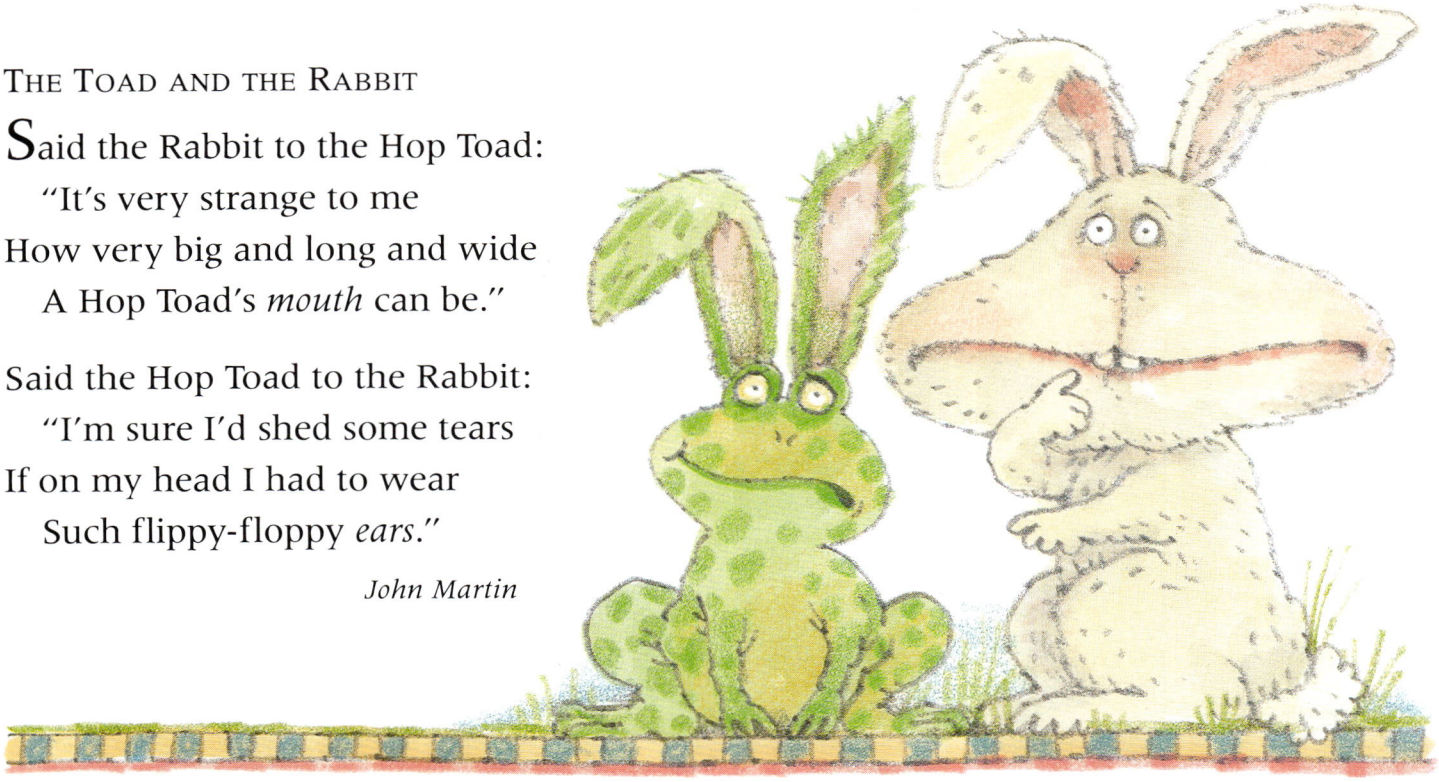

Good-Morning

One day I saw a downy duck,
With feathers on his back;
I said, "Good-morning, downy duck,"
And he said, "Quack, quack, quack."

One day I saw a timid mouse,
He was so shy and meek;
I said, "Good-morning, timid mouse,"
And he said, "Squeak, squeak, squeak."

One day I saw a curly dog,
I met him with a bow;
I said, "Good-morning, curly dog,"
And he said, "Bow-wow-wow."

One day I saw a scarlet bird,
He woke me from my sleep;
I said, "Good-morning, scarlet bird,"
And he said, "Cheep, cheep, cheep."

Muriel Sipe

Skeleton Parade

The skeletons are out tonight,
They march about the street
With bony bodies, bony heads
And bony hands and feet.

Bony bony bony bones
with nothing in between,
Up and down and all around
They march on Halloween.

Jack Prelutsky

On Halloween

We mask our faces
and wear strange hats
and moan like witches
and screech like cats
and jump like goblins
and thump like elves
and almost manage
to scare *ourselves.*

Aileen Fisher

Bedtime Story

"Tell me a story,"
Says Witch's Child,

"About the Beast
So fierce and wild.

About a Ghost
That shrieks and groans,

A Skeleton
That rattles bones,

About a Monster
Crawly-creepy.

Something nice
To make me sleepy."

Lilian Moore

Mix a Pancake

Mix a pancake,
Stir a pancake,
Pop it in the pan;
Fry the pancake,
Toss the pancake–
Catch it if you can.

Christina Rossetti

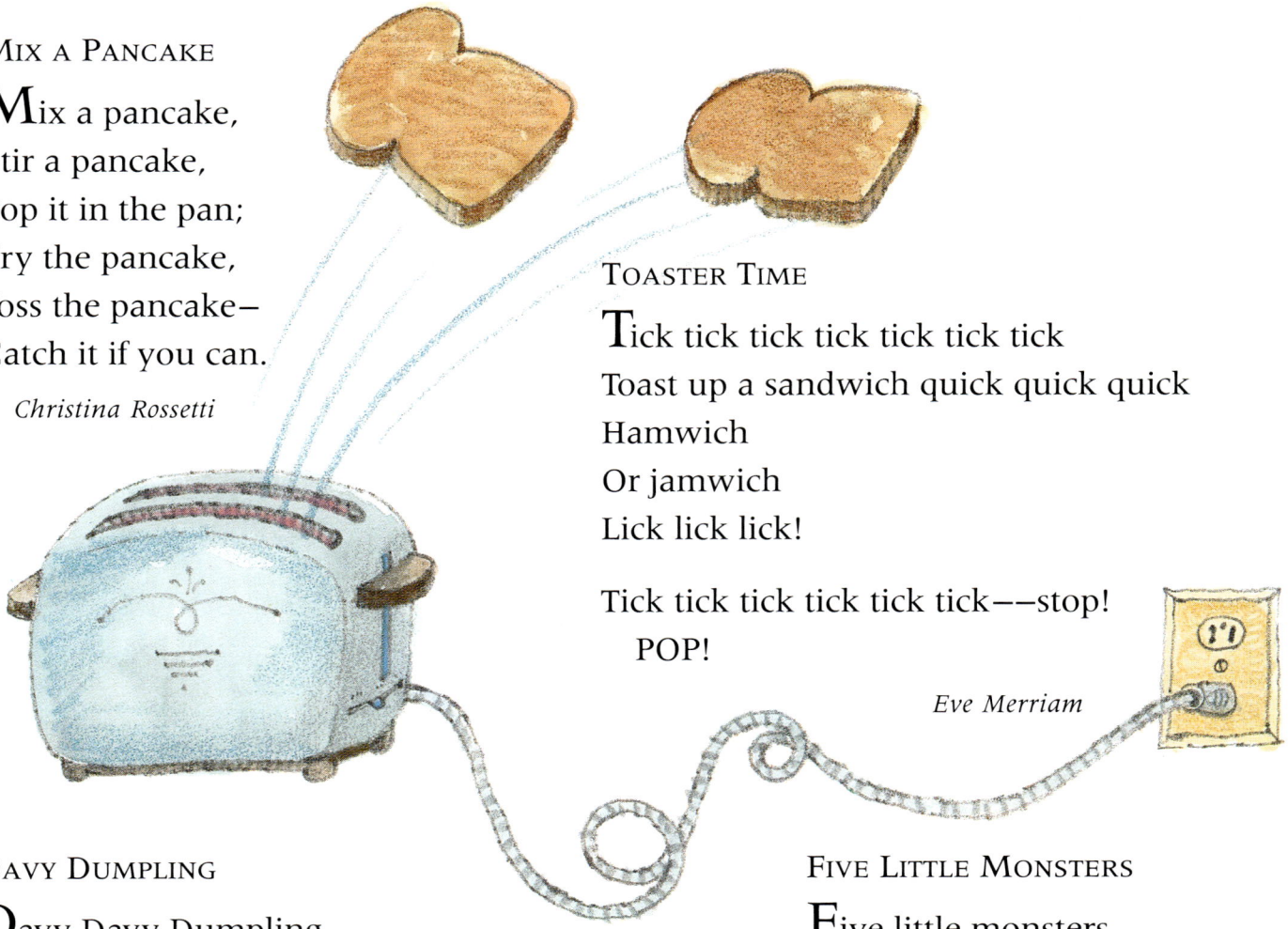

Toaster Time

Tick tick tick tick tick tick tick
Toast up a sandwich quick quick quick
Hamwich
Or jamwich
Lick lick lick!

Tick tick tick tick tick tick––stop!
POP!

Eve Merriam

Davy Dumpling

Davy Davy Dumpling,
Boil him in the pot;
Sugar him and butter him,
And eat him while he's hot.

Anonymous

Five Little Monsters

Five little monsters
By the light of the moon
Stirring pudding with
A wooden pudding spoon.
The first one says,
"It mustn't be runny."
The second one says,
"That would make it taste funny."
The third one says,
"It mustn't be lumpy."
The fourth one says,
"That would make me grumpy."
The fifth one smiles,
Hums a little tune,
And licks all the drippings
From the wooden pudding spoon.

Eve Merriam

The Wind and the Moon

Said the Wind to the Moon,
"I will blow you out;
You stare
In the air
Like a ghost in a chair
Always looking what I am about.
I hate to be watched—I'll blow you
out."

George MacDonald

The Moon's the North Wind's Cooky

The Moon's the North Wind's cooky.
He bites it, day by day,
Until there's but a rim of scraps
That crumble all away.

The South Wind is a baker.
He kneads clouds in his den,
And bakes a crisp new moon *that . . . greedy*
North . . . Wind . . . eats . . . again!

Vachel Lindsay

The Mistletoe

Mommy,
Daddy,
quick!
Let's go
and stand
beneath
the mistletoe.

You kiss me
and I'll kiss you,
here comes Sister,
kiss her too.

Mommy,
Daddy,
quick!
Let's go
and stand
beneath
the mistletoe.

Jack Prelutsky

December

All the months go past
  Each is like a guest;
December is the last,
  December is the best.

Each has lovely things,
  Each one is a friend,
But December brings
  Christmas at the end.

Rose Fyleman

Dreidel Song

Twirl about, dance about,
  Spin, spin, spin!
Turn, Dreidel, turn–
  Time to begin!

Soon it is Hanukkah–
  Fast, Dreidel, fast!
For you will lie still
  When Hanukkah's past.

Efraim Rosenzweig

My Teddy Bear

A teddy bear is a faithful friend.
You can pick him up at either end.
His fur is the color of breakfast toast,
And he's always there when you need him most.

Marchette Chute

My Teddy Bear

A teddy bear is nice to hold.
The one I have is getting old.
His paws are almost wearing out
And so's his funny furry snout
From rubbing on my nose of skin,
And all his fur is pretty thin.
A ribbon and a piece of string
Make a sort of necktie thing.
His eyes came out and now instead
He has some new ones made of thread.
I take him everywhere I go
And tell him all the things I know.
I like the way he feels at night,
All snuggled up against me tight.

Margaret Hillert

Teddy Bear, Teddy Bear

Teddy Bear, Teddy Bear,
Go upstairs.
Teddy Bear, Teddy Bear,
Say your prayers.
Teddy Bear, Teddy Bear,
Turn out the light.
Teddy Bear, Teddy Bear,
Say good night.

Anonymous

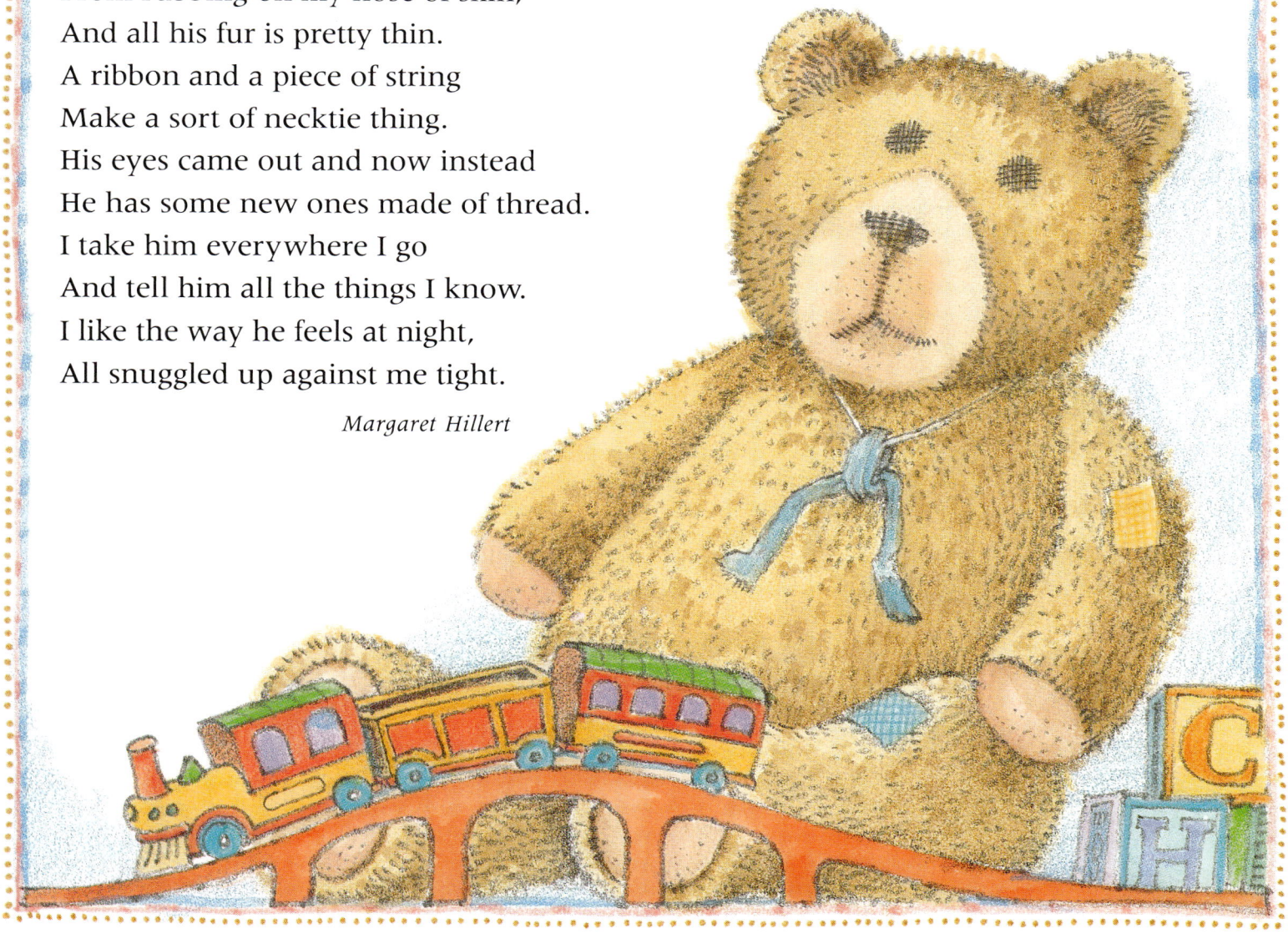

Cats and Dogs

Some like cats, and some like dogs,
and both of course are nice
if cats and dogs are what you want
–but I myself like mice.

For dogs chase cats, and cats chase rats
I guess they think it's fun.
I like my mouse the most because
he won't chase anyone.

N. M. Bodecker

Just Three

How very quiet things can be,
With just the dog, the cat, and me.
There's no one else to laugh and shout,
To dance and sing and run about.
With just the dog, the cat, and me,
How very quiet things can be.

William Wise

Hamsters

Hamsters are the nicest things
That anyone could own.
I like them even better than
Some dogs that I have known.

Their fur is soft, their faces nice.
They're small when they are grown.
And they sit inside your pocket
When you are all alone.

Marci Ridlon

Peter and Wendy

My ducks are so funny, I think.
They peck at the bugs in the ground,
And always wherever they go
They follow each other around.

They like to play Follow the Leader.
Just watch them awhile and you'll find
There's one of them always in front,
The other one always behind.

Wymond Garthwaite

Unfortunately

Dinosaurs lived so long ago,
they never had a chance to know
how many kids would love to get
a dinosaur to be their pet.

Bobbi Katz

Ode to Spring

O spring, O spring,
You wonderful thing!
O spring, O spring, O spring!
O spring, O spring,
When the birdies sing
I feel like a king,
O spring!

Walter R. Brooks

The Spring Wind

The summer wind
is soft and sweet
the winter wind is strong
the autumn wind is mischievous
and sweeps the leaves along.

The wind I love the best
comes gently after rain
smelling of spring and growing things
brushing the world with feathery wings
while everything glistens, and everything sings
in the spring wind
after the rain.

Charlotte Zolotow

Pussy Willows

Close your eyes
and do not peek
and I'll rub Spring
across your cheek–
smooth as satin,
soft and sleek–
close your eyes
and do not peek.

Aileen Fisher

Some Things That Easter Brings

Easter duck and Easter chick,
Easter eggs with chocolate thick.

Easter hats for one and all,
Easter Bunny makes a call!

Happy Easter always brings
Such a lot of pleasant things.

Elsie Parrish

The Squirrel

Whisky, frisky
Hippity hop,
Up he goes
To the treetop!

Whirly, twirly,
Round and round,
Down he scampers
To the ground.

Furly, curly,
What a tail!
Tall as a feather,
Broad as a sail!

Where's his supper?
In the shell,
Snappity, crackity,
Out it fell!

Anonymous

Giraffes Don't Huff

Giraffes don't huff or hoot or howl
They never grump, they never growl
They never roar, they never riot,
They eat green leaves
And just keep quiet.

Karla Kuskin

In the Summer We Eat

In the summer we eat,
in the winter we don't;
In the summer we'll play,
in the winter we won't.
All winter we sleep, each curled in a ball
As soon as the snowflakes start to fall.
But in spring we each come out of our den
And start to eat all over again.

Zhenya Gay

Johnny

To Johnny a box
is a house
or a car
or a ship
or a train
or a horse.
A stick
is a sword
or a spear
or a cane,
and a carpet
is magic,
of course.

Marci Ridlon

Yesterday's Paper

Yesterday's paper makes a hat,
Or a boat,
Or a plane,
Or a playhouse mat.
Yesterday's paper makes things
Like that–
And a very fine tent
For a sleeping cat.

Mabel Watts

Raindrops

How brave a ladybug must be!
Each drop of rain is big as she.

Can you imagine what *you'd* do
if raindrops fell as big as you?

Aileen Fisher

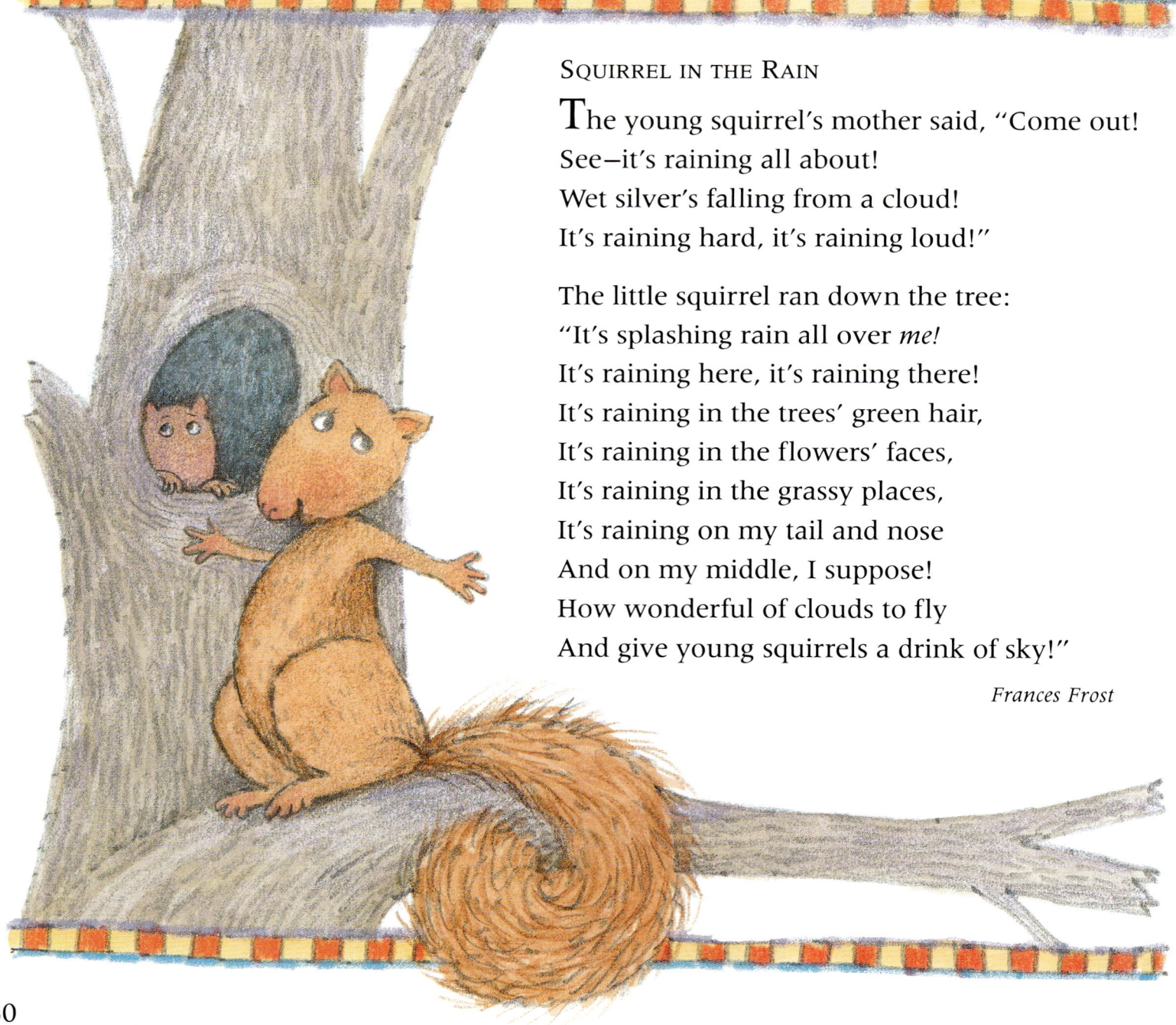

Squirrel in the Rain

The young squirrel's mother said, "Come out!
See—it's raining all about!
Wet silver's falling from a cloud!
It's raining hard, it's raining loud!"

The little squirrel ran down the tree:
"It's splashing rain all over *me!*
It's raining here, it's raining there!
It's raining in the trees' green hair,
It's raining in the flowers' faces,
It's raining in the grassy places,
It's raining on my tail and nose
And on my middle, I suppose!
How wonderful of clouds to fly
And give young squirrels a drink of sky!"

Frances Frost

Umbrellas

Umbrellas bloom
Along our street
Like flowers on a stem.
And almost everyone
I meet
Is holding one of them.

Under my umbrella-top,
Splashing through the town,
I wonder why the tulips
Hold umbrellas
Up-side-down!

Barbara Juster Esbensen

April

Rain is good
for washing leaves
and stones and bricks and
even eyes,
and if you hold
your head just so
you can almost see
the tops of skies.

Lucille Clifton

Only My Opinion

Is a caterpillar ticklish?
Well, it's always my belief
That he giggles, as he wiggles
Across a hairy leaf.

Monica Shannon

Fuzzy Wuzzy, Creepy Crawly

Fuzzy wuzzy, creepy crawly
Caterpillar funny,
You will be a butterfly
When the days are sunny.

Winging, flinging, dancing, springing
Butterfly so yellow,
You were once a caterpillar,
Wiggly, wiggly fellow.

Lillian Schulz

Ants Live Here

Ants live here
by the curb stone,
see?
They worry a lot
about giants like
me.

Lilian Moore

Ants

I like to watch the ants at work
When I am out at play.
I like to see them run about
And carry crumbs away.

And when I plug an anthill door
To keep them in their den,
I like to see them find a way
To get outside again.

Mary Ann Hoberman

Dragonfly

A dragonfly
  Is very thin,
Straight and shining,
  Like a pin,

With narrow wings
  Of stiffened gauze,
And in the air
  He likes to pause

And look at you
  With popping eyes.
He shimmers like
  A small surprise.

Florence Page Jaques

Grasshopper Green

Grasshopper green
Too quick to be seen
Jump like a Mexican jumpity bean!

Grasshopper high
Grasshopper low
Over my basket of berries you go!

Grasshopper low
Grasshopper high
Watch it or you will end up in a pie!

Nancy Dingman Watson

But I Wonder . . .

The crickets in the thickets,
and the katydids in trees,
and ants on plants, and butterflies,
and ladybugs and bees
don't smell with little noses
but with *feelers,* if you please.
They get along quite nicely,
but I wonder how they *sneeze.*

Aileen Fisher

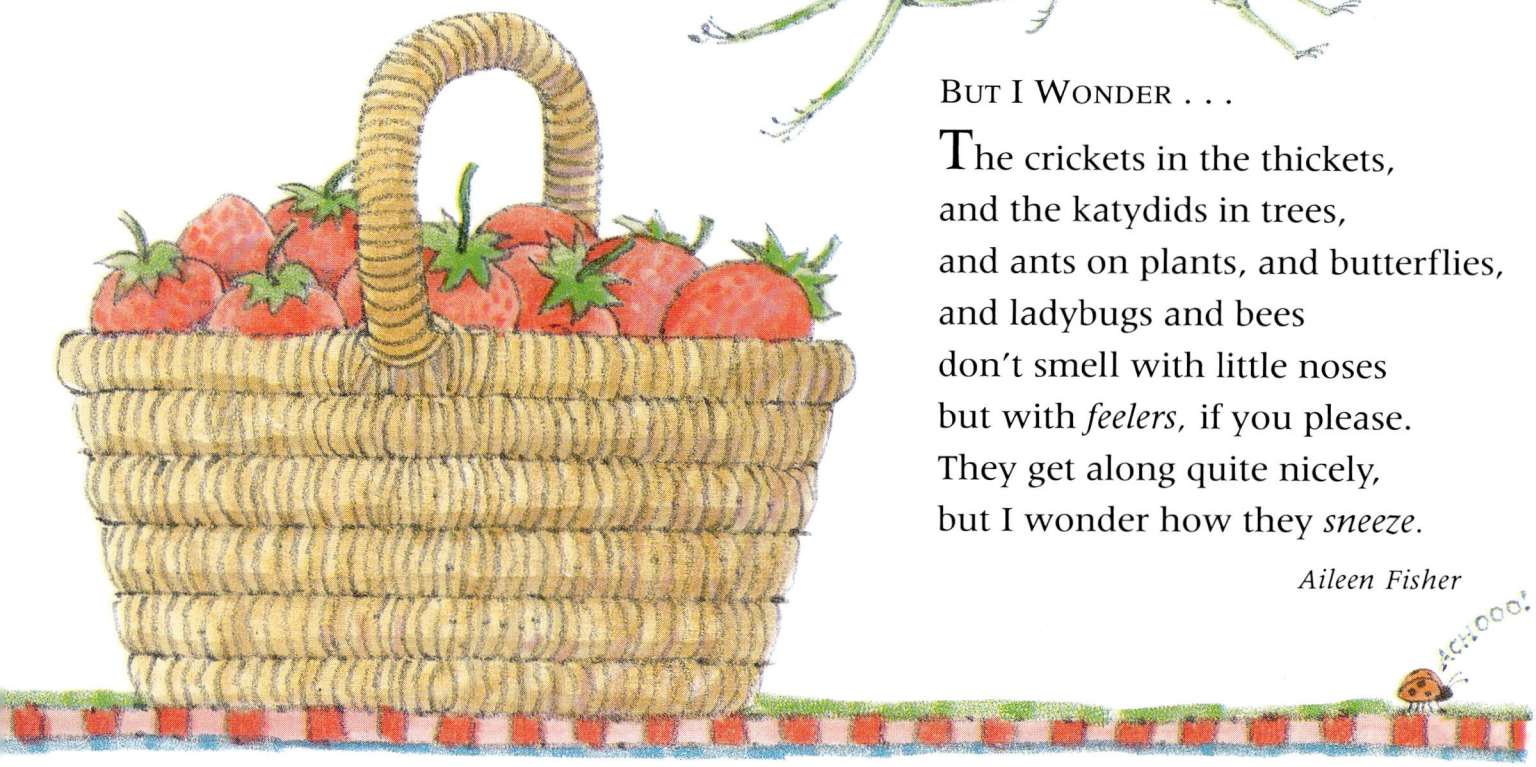

When All the World's Asleep

Where do insects go at night,
When all the world's asleep?
Where do bugs and butterflies
And caterpillars creep?
Turtles sleep inside their shells;
The robin has her nest.
Rabbits and the sly old fox
Have holes where they can rest.
Bears can crawl inside a cave;
The lion has his den.
Cows can sleep inside the barn,
And pigs can use their pen.
But where do bugs and butterflies
And caterpillars creep,
When everything is dark outside
And all the world's asleep?

Anita E. Posey

Night Comes . . .

Night comes
leaking
out of the sky.

Stars come
peeking.

Moon comes
sneaking,
silvery-sly.

Who is
shaking,
shivery-
quaking?

Who is afraid
of the night?

Not I.

Beatrice Schenk de Regniers

Firefly

A little light is going by,
Is going up to see the sky,
A little light with wings.

I never could have thought of it,
To have a little bug all lit
And made to go on wings.

Elizabeth Madox Roberts

Sleeping Outdoors

Under the dark is a star,
Under the star is a tree,
Under the tree is a blanket,
And under the blanket is me.

Marchette Chute

Covers

Glass covers windows
to keep the cold away
Clouds cover the sky
to make a rainy day

Nighttime covers
all the things that creep
Blankets cover me
when I'm asleep

Nikki Giovanni

Pretending

When you are in bed and it's cold outside,
do you ever pretend that you have to hide?
Do you curl up your toes?
Do you wrinkle your nose?
Do you make yourself little so none of you shows?

Do you pull the sheet over the whole of your face
and pretend you are in some faraway place?
Mother thinks you are sleeping,
but she does not know
that all tucked in your bed, you have places to go.

Bobbi Katz

Crunch and Lick

Popcorn crunches.
Peanuts do.
The cone part of an ice-cream cone
Is wonderful for crunching too.

Things to lick are candy sticks.
Rainbow-colored popsicles.
Chocolate sauce when it begins
To leak and trickle
Down our chins.

Dorothy Aldis

Yellow Butter

Yellow butter purple jelly red jam black bread

Spread it thick
Say it quick

Yellow butter purple jelly red jam black bread

Spread it thicker
Say it quicker

Yellow butter purple jelly red jam black bread

Now repeat it
While you eat it

Yellow butter purple jelly red jam black bread

Don't talk
With your mouth full!

Mary Ann Hoberman

The Meal

Timothy Tompkins had turnips and tea.
The turnips were tiny.
He ate at least three.
And then, for dessert,
He had onions and ice.
He liked that so much
That he ordered it twice.
He had two cups of ketchup,
A prune, and a pickle.
"Delicious," said Timothy.
"Well worth a nickel."
He folded his napkin
And hastened to add,
"It's one of the loveliest breakfasts I've had."

Karla Kuskin

Two Sad

It's such a shock, I almost screech,
When I find a worm inside my peach!
But then, what *really* makes me blue
Is to find a worm who's bit in two!

William Cole

Table Manners

The Goops they lick their fingers,
And the Goops they lick their knives;
They spill their broth on the tablecloth–
Oh, they lead disgusting lives!
The Goops they talk while eating,
And loud and fast they chew;
And that is why I'm glad that I
Am not a Goop–are you?

Gelett Burgess

Toothsome

No need to squeeze out half a tube
Of toothpaste, honeybunch–
Unless you plan to use it in
a sandwich for your lunch?

Norah Smaridge

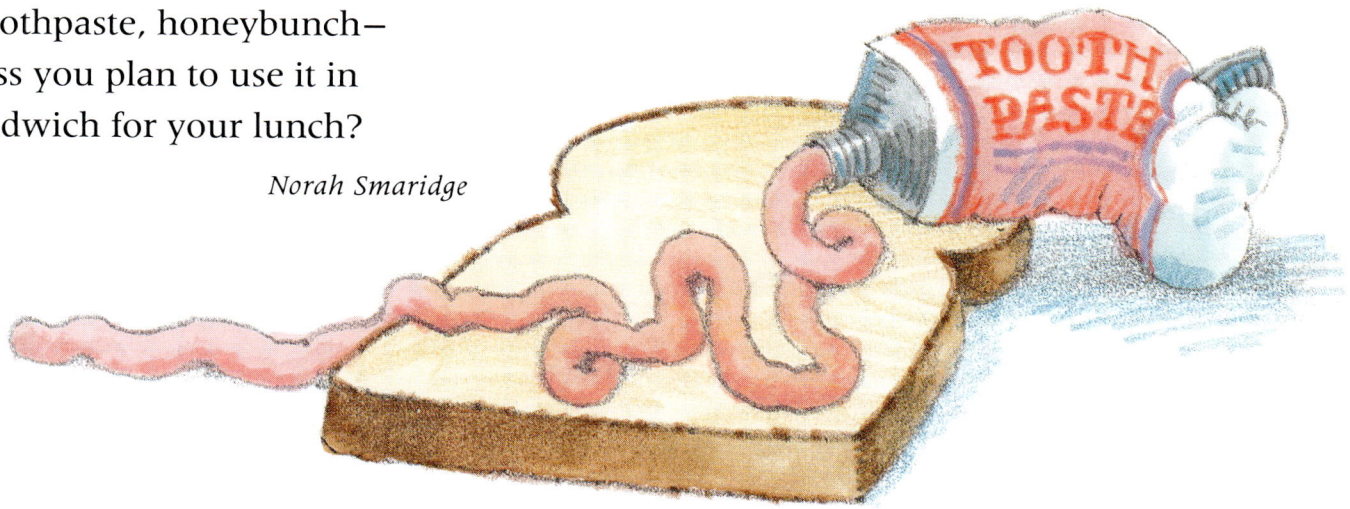

Night Fun

I hear eating.
I hear drinking.
I hear music.
I hear laughter.
Fun is something
Grownups never have
Before my bedtime.
Only after.

Judith Viorst

Bedtime

Five minutes, five minutes more, please!
  Let me stay five minutes more!
Can't I just finish the castle
  I'm building here on the floor?
Can't I just finish the story
  I'm reading here in my book?
Can't I just finish this bead-chain–
  It *almost* is finished, look!
Can't I just finish this game, please?
  When a game's once begun
It's a pity never to find out
  Whether you've lost or won.
Can't I just stay five minutes?
  Well, can't I stay just four?
Three minutes, then? two minutes?
  Can't I stay *one* minute more?

Eleanor Farjeon

Moon Boat

Moon Boat, little, brave and bright,
Tossed upon the seas of night,
One day when I'm free to roam,
I'll climb aboard and steer you home.

Charlotte Pomerantz

I See the Moon

I see the moon,
And the moon sees me;
God bless the moon,
And God bless me.

Anonymous

Moon-Come-Out

Moon-Come-Out
And Sun-Go-In,
Here's a soft blanket
To cuddle your chin.

Moon-Go-In
And Sun-Come-Out,
Throw off the blanket
And bustle about.

Eleanor Farjeon

The Star

Twinkle, twinkle, little star,
How I wonder what you are!
Up above the world so high,
Like a diamond in the sky.

As your bright and tiny spark,
Lights the traveler in the dark–
Though I know not what you are,
Twinkle, twinkle, little star.

Jane Taylor

The Little Elf

I met a little Elf man, once,
Down where the lilies blow.
I asked him why he was so small,
And why he didn't grow.

He slightly frowned, and with his eye
He looked me through and through.
"I'm quite as big for me," said he,
"As you are big for you."

John Kendrick Bangs

An Explanation of the Grasshopper

The Grasshopper, the Grasshopper,
I will explain to you:
He is the Brownies' racehorse,
The Fairies' Kangaroo.

Vachel Lindsay

Fairies

Don't go looking for fairies,
They'll fly away if you do.
You never can see the fairies
Till they come looking for you.

Eleanor Farjeon

Under the Ground

What is under the grass,
Way down in the ground,
Where everything is cool and wet
With darkness all around?

Little pink worms live there;
Ants and brown bugs creep
Softly round the stones and rocks
Where roots are pushing deep.

Do they hear us walking
On the grass above their heads;
Hear us running over
While they snuggle in their beds?

Rhoda W. Bacmeister

The Underworld

When I am lying in the grass
I watch the ants and beetles pass;
And once I lay so very still
A mole beside me built a hill.

Margaret Lavington

Dragon Smoke

Breathe and blow
white clouds
with every puff.
It's cold today,
cold enough
to see your breath.
Huff!
Breathe dragon smoke
today!

Lilian Moore

The Mitten Song

"Thumbs in the thumb-place,
Fingers all together!"
This is the song
We sing in mitten-weather.
When it is cold,
It doesn't matter whether
Mittens are wool,
Or made of finest leather–
This is the song
We sing in mitten-weather:
"Thumbs in the thumb-place,
Fingers all together!"

Marie Louise Allen

The More It Snows

The more it
SNOWS-tiddely-pom,
The more it
GOES-tiddely-pom
The more it
GOES-tiddely-pom
On
Snowing.

And nobody
KNOWS-tiddely-pom,
How cold my
TOES-tiddely-pom
How cold my
TOES-tiddely-pom
Are
Growing.

A. A. Milne

Winter Sweetness

This little house is sugar.
Its roof with snow is piled,
And from its tiny window
Peeps a maple-sugar child.

Langston Hughes

Jack Frost

Someone painted pictures on my
Window pane last night–
Willow trees with trailing boughs
And flowers–frosty white
And lovely crystal butterflies;
But when the morning sun
Touched them with its golden beams,
They vanished one by one!

Helen Bayley Davis

It Fell in the City

It fell in the city,
It fell through the night,
And the black rooftops
All turned white.

Red fire hydrants
All turned white.
Blue police cars
All turned white.

Green garbage cans
All turned white.
Gray sidewalks
All turned white.

Yellow NO PARKING signs
All turned white
When it fell in the city
All through the night.

Eve Merriam

First Snow

Snow makes whiteness where it falls.
The bushes look like popcorn-balls.
And places where I always play,
Look like somewhere else today.

Marie Louise Allen

Icy

I slip and I slide
On the slippery ice;
I skid and I glide–
Oh, isn't it nice
To lie on your tummy
And slither and skim
On the slick crust of snow
Where you skid as you swim?

Rhoda W. Bacmeister

January

In January
it's so nice
while slipping
on the sliding ice
to sip hot chicken soup
with rice.
Sipping once
sipping twice
sipping chicken soup
with rice.

Maurice Sendak

Snowman

My little snowman has a mouth,
So he is always smiling south.
My little snowman has a nose;
I couldn't seem to give him toes,
I couldn't seem to make his ears.
He shed a lot of frozen tears
Before I gave him any eyes–
But they are big ones for his size.

David McCord

Snow

We'll play in the snow
And stray in the snow
And stay in the snow
In a snow-white park.
We'll clown in the snow
And frown in the snow
Fall down in the snow
Till it's after dark.
We'll cook snow pies
In a big snow pan.
We'll make snow eyes
In a round snow man.
We'll sing snow songs
And chant snow chants
And roll in the snow
In our fat snow pants.
And when it's time to go home to eat
We'll have snow toes
On our frosted feet.

Karla Kuskin

If I Were Bigger Than Anyone

If I were bigger than anyone,
If I were taller than trees,
I could step over hills and towns
And go anywhere I please.

If I got bored with being huge,
The next day I'd be small.
But the size I really am
I might not choose at all.

Ruth Harnden

Open House

If I were a tree
I'd want to see
a bird with a song
on a branch of me.

I'd want a quick
little squirrel to run
up and down
and around, for fun.

I'd want the cub
of a bear to call,
a porcupine, big,
and a tree-toad, small.

I'd want a katydid
out of sight
on one of my leaves
to sing at night.

And down by my roots
I'd want a mouse
with six little mouselings
in her house.

Aileen Fisher

I'd Like to Be a Lighthouse

I'd like to be a lighthouse
  All scrubbed and painted white.
I'd like to be a lighthouse
  And stay awake all night
To keep my eye on everything
  That sails my patch of sea;
I'd like to be a lighthouse
  With the ships all watching me.

Rachel Field

Tell Me Little Woodworm

Tell me little woodworm
Eating through the wood
Surely all that sawdust
Can't do you any good.

Heavens! Little woodworm
You've eaten all the chairs
So *that's* why poor old Grandad's
Sitting outside on the stairs.

Spike Milligan

Three Tickles

Pizza, pickle,
Pumpernickel,
My little guy
Shall have a tickle:

One for his nose,
And one for his toes,
And one for his tummy
Where the hot dog goes.

Dennis Lee

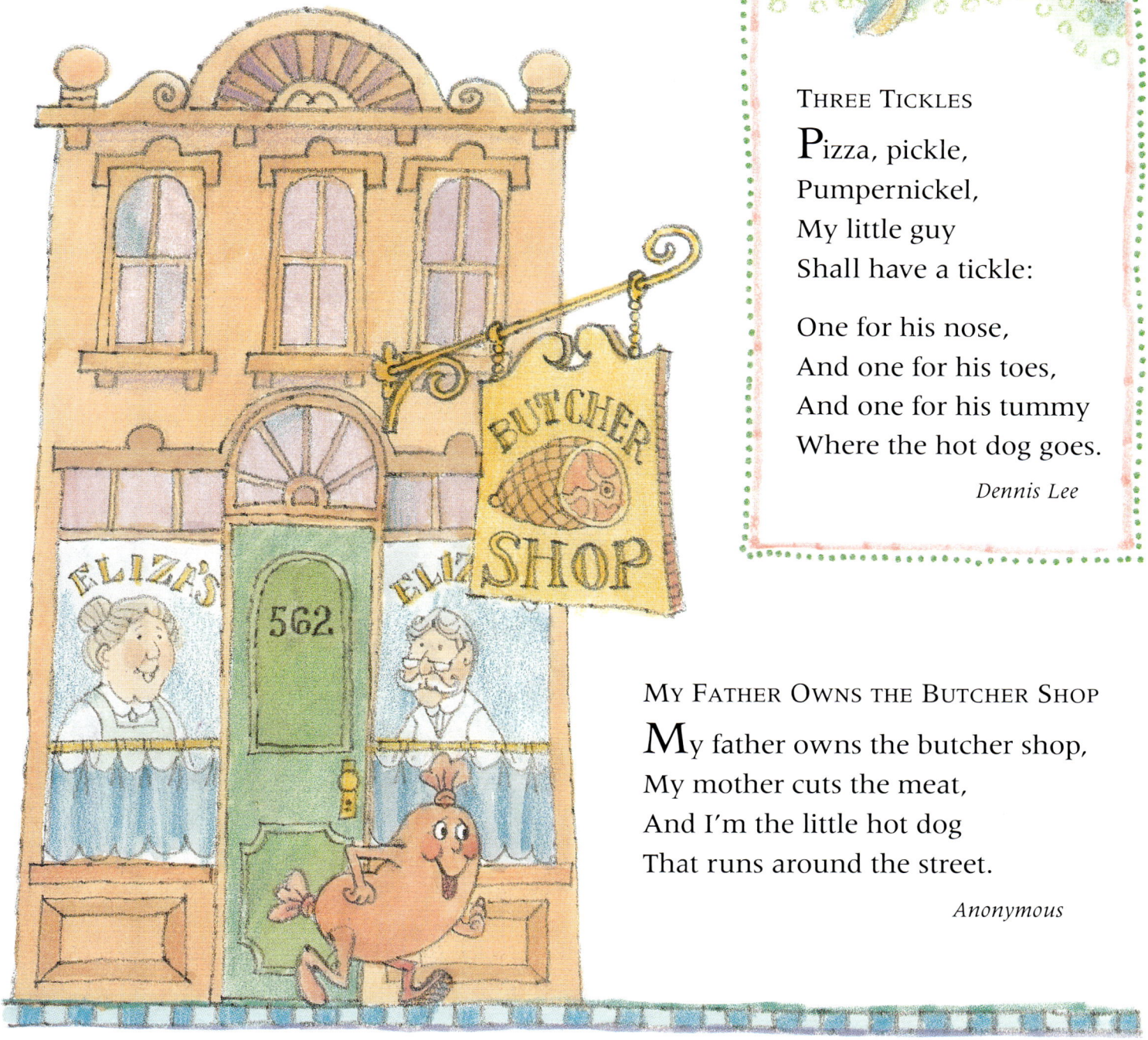

My Father Owns the Butcher Shop

My father owns the butcher shop,
My mother cuts the meat,
And I'm the little hot dog
That runs around the street.

Anonymous

Runaway

I think today
I'll run away.
My heart is filled with sorrow.

I'll disappear
For one whole year,
Or else, come back tomorrow.

William Wise

Sometimes

Sometimes I simply have to cry,
I don't know why,
I don't know why.
There's really nothing very wrong,
I probably should sing a song
or run around and make some noise
or sit and tinker with my toys
or pop a couple of balloons
or play a game or watch cartoons,
but I'm feeling sad,
though I don't know why,
and all I want to do is cry.

Jack Prelutsky

It's Eleven O'clock

It's eleven o'clock
and there's nothing to do
but stand on one leg
and then stand on two.

Eleven o'clock–
it's not a nice hour.
It's boring and hungry
and heavy and sour.

Nancy Chambers

Someone's Face

Someone's face was all frowned shut,
All squeezed full of grims and crinkles,
Pouts and scowls and gloomers, but
I could see behind the wrinkles–

Even with her face a-twist,
I saw Someone peeking through.
And when Someone's nose was kissed,
Guess who came out giggling?–YOU!

John Ciardi

Robert, Who Is Often a Stranger to Himself

Do you ever look in the looking-glass
And see a stranger there?
A child you know and do not know,
Wearing what you wear?

Gwendolyn Brooks

Ten Fingers

I have ten little fingers
And they all belong to me.
I can make them do things.
Would you like to see?
I can shut them up tight
Or open them wide.
I can put them together
Or make them all hide.
I can make them jump high,
I can make them jump low,
I can fold them quietly
And hold them just so.

Anonymous

Wide Awake

I have to jump up
out of bed
and stretch my hands
and rub my head,
and curl my toes
and yawn
and shake
myself
all wide-awake!

Myra Cohn Livingston

Here All We See

Here all we see
Is Ann's small nose,
A smile, two legs,
And ten pink toes,
Neatly arranged
In two short rows.

Walter de la Mare

Somersaults

It's fun turning somersaults
and bouncing on the bed,
I walk on my hands
and I stand on my head.

I swing like a monkey
and I tumble and I shake,
I stretch and I bend,
but I never never break.

I wiggle like a worm
and I wriggle like an eel,
I hop like a rabbit
and I flop like a seal.

I leap like a frog
and I jump like a flea,
there must be rubber
inside of me.

Jack Prelutsky

EARS HEAR

Flies buzz,
Motors roar.
Kettles hiss,
People snore.
Dogs bark,
Birds cheep.
Autos honk: *Beep! Beep!*

Winds sigh,
Shoes squeak.
Trucks honk,
Floors creak.
Whistles toot,
Bells clang.
Doors slam: *Bang! Bang!*

Kids shout,
Clocks ding.
Babies cry,
Phones ring.
Balls bounce,
Spoons drop.
People scream: *Stop! Stop!*

Lucia and James L. Hymes, Jr.

Sneeze

There's a
sort of a
tickle
the size of a
nickel,
a bit like the
prickle
of sweet-sour
pickle;

it's a
quivery
shiver
the shape of a
sliver,
like eels in a
river;

a kind of a
wiggle
that starts as a
jiggle
and joggles
its way to a
tease,

which I
cannot
suppress
any longer,
I guess,
so pardon me,
please,
while I
sneeze.

Maxine Kumin

Drinking Fountain

When I climb up
To get a drink,
It doesn't work
The way you'd think.

I turn it up,
The water goes
And hits me right
Upon the nose.

I turn it down
To make it small
And don't get any
Drink at all.

Marchette Chute

Crayons

I've colored a picture with crayons.
  I'm not very pleased with the sun.
I'd like it much stronger and brighter
  And more like the actual one.
I've tried with the crayon that's yellow,
  I've tried with the crayon that's red.
But none of it looks like the sunlight
  I carry around in my head.

Marchette Chute

Keziah

I have a secret place to go.
Not anyone may know.

And sometimes when the wind is rough
I cannot get there fast enough.

And sometimes when my mother
Is scolding my big brother,

My secret place, it seems to me,
Is quite the only place to be.

Gwendolyn Brooks

The Evening Is Coming

The evening is coming.
The sun sinks to rest.
The birds are all flying
straight home to their nests.
"Caw, caw," says the crow
as he flies overhead.
It's time little children
were going to bed.

Here comes the pony.
His work is all done.
Down through the meadow
he takes a good run.
Up go his heels,
and down goes his head.
It's time little children
were going to bed.

Anonymous

Silverly

Silverly,
Silverly,
Over the
Trees
The moon drifts
By on a
Runaway
Breeze.

Dozily,
Dozily,
Deep in her
Bed,
A little girl
Dreams with the
Moon in her
Head.

Dennis Lee

Hushabye My Darling

Hushabye my darling
Don't you make a peep
Little creatures everywhere
Are settling down to sleep

Fishes in the millpond
Goslings in the barn
Kitten by the fireside
Baby in my arms

Listen to the raindrops
Singing you to sleep
Hushabye my darling
Don't you make a peep

Clyde Watson

Good Night, Good Night

The dark is dreaming.
Day is done.
Good night, good night
To everyone.

Good night to the birds,
And the fish in the sea,
Good night to the bears
And good night to me.

Dennis Lee

Index of Titles

Ants, 62
Ants Live Here, 62
April, 61
At Night, 18
August Heat, 32

Baby's Baking, 30
Bedtime, 70
Bedtime Story, 49
Before the Bath, 26
Before the Monkey's Cage, 22
Belly & Tubs Went Out in a Boat, 45
Big, 28
Big Turtle, A, 20
Birthdays, 29
Blowing Bubbles, 9
But I Wonder . . . , 63
Butterfly, The, 33

Cat Kisses, 18
Cats and Dogs, 54
Chook, Chook, 42
Chums, 40
Covers, 66
Crayons, 86
Crunch and Lick, 67

Dangerous, 9
Davy Dumpling, 50
December, 52
Donkey, The, 46
Dragon Smoke, 74
Dragonfly, 63
Dreadful Doings of Jelly Belly, The, 45
Dreidel Song, 52
Drinking Fountain, 85
Ducks in the Rain, 43

Ears Hear, 84
Elephant Carries a Great Big Trunk, The, 10
Evening Is Coming, The, 87
Explanation of the Grasshopper, An, 72

Fairies, 72
Firefly, 65
First Snow, 76
Fish, 44
Fish, 44
Five Little Chickens, 42
Five Little Monsters, 50
Five Years Old, 29
Footnote, 8
Frog and a Flea, A, 4
Frog on the Log, The, 21
Fun, 47
Fuzzy Wuzzy, Creepy Crawly, 62

Giraffes Don't Huff, 58
Gold-Tinted Dragon, The, 34
Good-Morning, 48
Good Neighbors, 24
Good Night, Good Night, 88
Grasshopper Green, 63

Halfway Down, 15
Hamsters, 54
Happy Thought, 39
Happy Winter, Steamy Tub, 27
Here All We See, 82
Hide and Seek, 8
Hide-and-Seek Shadow, 25
Higglety, Pigglety, Pop! 5
Holding Hands, 11
Home, 30
House Cat, The, 18
House Mouse, The, 24
How a Puppy Grows, 40
Humming Birds, 23
Huntsmen, The, 45
Hushabye My Darling, 87

I Can Be a Tiger, 17
I See the Moon, 71
Icy, 76
I'd Like to Be a Lighthouse, 78
If I Were Bigger Than Anyone, 78
In the Summer We Eat, 58
It Fell in the City, 75
It's Eleven O'Clock, 80

Jack Frost, 75
January, 76
Johnny, 59
Joyful, 32
Jump or Jiggle, 7
Just Three, 54
Just Watch, 6

Keziah, 86
Kite, A, 33

Little Elf, The, 72
Little Seeds, 14
Little Talk, A, 43
Little Turtle, The, 20
Little Wind, 12
Look, 25

Makers, 39
Mary Middling, 36
Meal, The, 68
Mice, 24
Mistletoe, The, 52
Mitten Song, The, 74
Mix a Pancake, 50
Modern Dragon, A, 35
Moon Boat, 71
Moon-Come-Out, 71
Moon's the North Wind's Cooky, The, 51
More It Snows, The, 74
Mother Cat's Purr, 19
Mud, 13

My Dragon, 35
My Father Owns the Butcher Shop, 79
My Sister Laura, 28
My Teddy Bear, 53
My Teddy Bear, 53

Naughty Soap Song, 26
Night Comes . . . , 65
Night Fun, 70

Ode to Spring, 56
Old Person of Ware, An, 10
Old Woman, The, 24
On Halloween, 49
Only My Opinion, 62
Open House, 78

Peter and Wendy, 55
Picnic, The, 31
Picnic Day, 32
Pigs, The, 36
Polar Bear, 10
Poor Shadow, 25
Pretending, 66
Puppy Chased the Sunbeam, The, 40
Pussy Willows, 57

Quack, Quack! 43

Raggedy Dog, The, 4
Rain, The, 12
Raindrops, 60
Rainy Day, 13
Robert, Who Is Often a Stranger to Himself, 81
Run a Little, 5
Runaway, 80

Shore, 30
Showers, 12
Silverly, 87
Singing in the Spring, 23
Singing-Time, 3
Skeleton Parade, 49
Skyscraper, 41
Sleeping Outdoors, 65
Slippery Sam, 45
Snail and the Mouse, The, 4
Snail's Pace, 20
Sneeze, 85
Snow, 77
Snowman, 77
Some Things That Easter Brings, 57
Someone's Face, 81
Somersaults, 83
Something About Me, 28
Sometimes, 80
Spike of Green, A, 14
Spring Wind, The, 56
Squirrel, The, 58
Squirrel in the Rain, 60
Star, The, 71
Sun After Rain, 13
Swallow, The, 23
Swimming, 9

Table Manners, 69
Teddy Bear, Teddy Bear, 53
Tell Me Little Woodworm, 79
Ten Fingers, 82
Ten to One, 37
There Was a Small Pig Who Wept Tears, 36
There's Music in a Hammer, 47
Three Tickles, 79
Toad, The, 21
Toad and the Rabbit, The, 48
Toaster, The, 35
Toaster Time, 50
Toothsome, 69
Top and the Tip, The, 38
Twinkle, Twinkle, 46
Two Sad, 68

Umbrellas, 61
Under the Ground, 73
Underworld, The, 73
Unfortunately, 55

Very Nicest Place, The, 38

Way Down South, 46
Way They Scrub, The, 27
We Built a Castle Near the Rocks, 31
When All the World's Asleep, 64
When You Talk to a Monkey, 22
Whistling, 6
Wide Awake, 82
Wild Beasts, 16
Wind and the Moon, The, 51
Wings, 39
Winter Sweetness, 74
Wish, 27
Wish, The, 29
Woodpecker in Disguise, 23
World, The, 28
Wouldn't You? 33

Yellow Butter, 67
Yesterday's Paper, 59

Index of First Lines

A big turtle sat on the end of a log, 20
A dragonfly, 63
A frog and a flea, 4
A little light is going by, 65
A little old woman, 24
A silver-scaled Dragon with jaws flaming red, 35
A summer day is full of ease, 32
A teddy bear is a faithful friend, 53
A teddy bear is nice to hold, 53
A train is a dragon that roars through the dark, 35
All the months go past, 52
Ants live here, 62
As I was walking along-long-long, 23

Bees have four wings, 39
Beetlebombs make jelly jam, 39
Belly & Tubs went out in a boat, 45
Breathe and blow, 74

Chook, chook, chook, chook, chook, 42
Close your eyes, 57

Davy Davy Dumpling, 50
Dinosaurs lived so long ago, 55
Dip your pipe and gently blow, 9
Do you ever look in the looking-glass, 81
Don't go looking for fairies, 72
Ducks are dabbling in the rain, 43

Each birthday wish, 29
Easter duck and Easter chick, 57
Elephants walking, 11
Everything has a shadow, 25

Firelight and shadows, 25
Five little monsters, 50
Five minutes, five minutes more, please! 70
Flies buzz, 84
Frogs jump, 7
Fuzzy wuzzy, creepy crawly, 62

Giraffes don't huff or hoot or howl, 58
Glass covers windows, 66
Grasshopper green, 63

Hair is the top of a person, 38
Halfway down the stairs, 15
Hamsters are the nicest things, 54
Happy Winter, steamy tub, 27
He sits and begs; he gives a paw, 40
Here all we see, 82
Higglety, pigglety, pop! 5
How brave a ladybug must be! 60
How very quiet things can be, 54
Hushabye my darling, 87

I can't go walking, 17
I do not like a rainy day, 13
I had a Donkey, that was all right, 46
I have a purple dragon, 35
I have a secret place to go, 86
I have ten little fingers, 82
I have to jump up, 82

I hear eating, 70
I like to watch the ants at work, 62
I love to hear a lobster laugh, 47
I met a little Elf man, once, 72
I met a little woman, 21
I often sit and wish that I, 33
I see the moon, 71
I slip and I slide, 76
I think it is a funny thing, 23
I think it's very funny, 40
I think mice, 24
I think today, 80
I wake in the morning early, 3
I walked with my shadow, 25
I will be a lion, 16
I'd like to be a lighthouse, 78
If birthdays happened once a week, 29
If I, 33
If I could wish, 27
If I were a tree, 78
If I were bigger than anyone, 78
In August, when the days are hot, 32
In January, 76
In the summer we eat, 58
Is a caterpillar ticklish? 62
Isn't it foolish to dash off outside, 8
It fell in the city, 75
It's cold, cold, cold, 26
It's eleven o'clock, 80
It's fun turning somersaults, 83
It's such a shock, I almost screech, 68
I've colored a picture with crayons, 86

Jelly Belly bit, 45
Just when I'm ready to, 26

Little brown house mouse, laugh and leap, 24
Little seeds we sow in spring, 14

Little wind, blow on the hill-top, 12
Look at them flit, 44

Mary Middling had a pig, 36
Maybe it's so, 20
Mix a pancake, 50
Mommy, 52
Moon Boat, little, brave and bright, 71
Moon-Come-Out, 71
Mud is very nice to feel, 13
My ducks are so funny, I think, 55
My father owns the butcher shop, 79
My little snowman has a mouth, 77
My sister Laura's bigger than me, 28

Night comes, 65
No need to squeeze out half a tube, 69
Now I can catch and throw a ball, 28

O spring, O spring, 56
Oh, I can laugh and I can sing, 6
One day I saw a downy duck, 48

Piggie Wig and Piggie Wee, 36
Pizza, pickle, 79
Play on the seashore, 30
Please, everybody, look at me! 29
Popcorn crunches, 67

Rain is good, 61
Rain on the green grass, 12
Rain, rain, 13
Run a little this way, 5

Said the first little chicken, 42
Said the Rabbit to the Hop Toad, 48
Said the Wind to the Moon, 51
Sandpaper kisses, 18
Silverly, 87
Sing a song of picnics, 32
Skyscraper, skyscraper, 41
Sleep the half-sleep, 19
Slippery Sam, 45

Snow makes whiteness where it falls, 76
So, so, spade and hoe, 30
Some like cats, and some like dogs, 54
Someone painted pictures on my, 75
Someone's face was all frowned shut, 81
Sometimes I simply have to cry, 80
Squelch and squirt and squiggle, 12
Swallow, swallow, swooping free, 23

Teddy Bear, Teddy Bear, 53
"Tell me a story," 49
Tell me little woodworm, 79
Ten tired tortoises, 37
The big brown hen and Mrs. Duck, 43
The crickets in the thickets, 63
The dark is dreaming, 88
The elephant carries a great big trunk, 10
The evening is coming, 87
The fish lives in the brook, 38
The Goops they lick their fingers, 69
The Grasshopper, the Grasshopper, 72
The house cat sits, 18
The little fish are silent, 44
The monkey curled his tail about, 22
The Moon's the North Wind's cooky, 51
The more it, 74
The puppy chased the sunbeam, 40
The Raggedy Dog chased the Raggedy Cat, 4
The sea is ringed around with hills, 30
The secret of the polar bear, 10
The skeletons are out tonight, 49
The Snail and the Mouse, 4
The summer wind, 56
The way they scrub, 27
The world is big, 28
The world is so full of a number of things, 39
The young squirrel's mother said, "Come out!" 60
There once, 21
There was a little turtle, 20
There was a small pig who wept tears, 36
There was an old person of Ware, 10
There's a, 85
There's music in a hammer, 47
There's something about me, 28
This little house is sugar, 74
Three jolly gentlemen, 45
"Thumbs in the thumb-place," 74
Tick tick tick tick tick tick tick, 50
Timothy Tompkins had turnips and tea, 68
To Johnny a box, 59
Twinkle, twinkle, little bat! 46
Twinkle, twinkle, little star, 71
Twirl about, dance about, 52

Umbrellas bloom, 61
Under the dark is a star, 65
Up and down the air you float, 33

Watch, 6
Watch me swim! 9
Way down South where bananas grow, 46
We brought a rug for sitting on, 31
We built a castle near the rocks, 31
We have two ducks. One blue. One black, 43
We mask our faces, 49
We'll play in the snow, 77
What is under the grass, 73
What's the good of a wagon, 34
When I am alone, and quite alone, 8
When I am lying in the grass, 73
When I climb up, 85
When I went out, 14
When night is dark, 18
When we're, 9
When you are in bed and it's cold outside, 66
When you talk to a monkey, 22
Where do insects go at night, 64
Whisky, frisky, 58
Woodpecker taps at the apple tree, 23

Yellow butter purple jelly red jam black bread, 67
Yesterday's paper makes a hat, 59
You know the old woman, 24

Index of Authors

Aldis, Dorothy, 9, 26, 28, 31, 67
Allen, Marie Louise, 29, 74, 76
Anderson, Mildred Leigh, 17
Anglund, Joan Walsh, 31

Bacmeister, Rhoda W., 73, 76
Baker, Barbara, 14
Bangs, John Kendrick, 72
Becker, Edna, 22
Bennett, Rowena, 22, 35
Beyer, Evelyn, 7
Bodecker, N.M., 54
Bourinot, Arthur S., 44
Boyden, Polly Chase, 13
Brooks, Gwendolyn, 81, 86
Brooks, Walter R., 56
Burgess, Gelett, 69
Burgunder, Rose, 32

Carroll, Lewis, 46
Chambers, Nancy, 80
Chute, Marchette, 12, 53, 65, 85, 86
Ciardi, John, 33, 81
Clifton, Lucille, 61
Coatsworth, Elizabeth, 21
Cole, William, 68

Davis, Helen Bayley, 75
De la Mare, Walter, 45, 82
De Regniers, Beatrice Schenk, 65

Eastwick, Ivy O., 23, 37, 40
Esbensen, Barbara Juster, 61

Farber, Norma, 13
Farjeon, Eleanor, 70, 71, 72
Field, Rachel, 32, 78
Fisher, Aileen, 18, 20, 39, 49, 57, 60, 63, 78
Friday, Ann, 29
Frost, Frances, 60
Fyleman, Rose, 3, 24, 36, 52

Garthwaite, Wymond, 55
Gay, Zhenya, 58
Giovanni, Nikki, 66
Goodrich, Samuel, 5
Greenaway, Kate, 12
Guiterman, Arthur, 40
Gundersheimer, Karen, 27

Hallock, Grace Taber, 23
Harnden, Ruth, 78
Higgins, Alice, 9
Hillert, Margaret, 9, 25, 53
Hoberman, Mary Ann, 29, 44, 62, 67
Hughes, Langston, 74
Hymes, Lucia, and James L., Jr., 84

Jackson, Leroy F., 40, 47
Jaques, Florence Page, 63
Jaszi, Jean, 30
Justus, May, 24

Katz, Bobbi, 18, 55, 66
Kennedy, X.J., 35
Kredenser, Gail, 10
Kumin, Maxine, 85
Kuskin, Karla, 34, 58, 68, 77

Lavington, Margaret, 73
Lear, Edward, 10
Lee, Dennis, 41, 45, 79, 87, 88
Lindsay, Vachel, 20, 51, 72
Link, Lenore M., 11
Livingston, Myra Cohn, 6, 82
Lobel, Arnold, 36

McCord, David, 77
MacDonald, George, 51
Marsh, Corinna, 26
Martin, John, 48
Merriam, Eve, 50, 75
Miller, Mary Britton, 30
Milligan, Spike, 28, 79
Milne, A.A., 15, 74
Minarik, Else Holmelund, 14
Mitchell, Cynthia, 4
Moore, Lilian, 49, 62, 74

Nash, Ogden, 23

Orleans, Ilo, 21, 25

Parrish, Elsie, 57
Pomerantz, Charlotte, 71
Posey, Anita E., 64
Potter, Beatrix, 24
Poulsson, Emilie, 36
Prelutsky, Jack, 6, 24, 49, 52, 80, 83

Reeves, James, 5
Richards, Laura E., 4
Ridlon, Marci, 54, 59
Ripley, Sherman, 4
Roberts, Elizabeth Madox, 65
Roethke, Theodore, 46
Rosenzweig, Efraim, 52
Ross, A.B., 27
Rossetti, Christina, 50

Sage, Betty, 23
Schulz, Lillian, 62
Scollard, Clinton, 33
Sendak, Maurice, 76
Seuss, Dr., 43
Shannon, Monica, 62
Shiffrin, A.B., 8
Sipe, Muriel, 48
Smaridge, Norah, 8, 69
Smith, William Jay, 35
Spilka, Arnold, 45
Stein, Evaleen, 16, 30
Stevenson, Robert Louis, 39

Taylor, Jane, 71
Thompson, Dorothy Brown, 27
Tippett, James S., 43

Viorst, Judith, 70

Watson, Clyde, 45, 87
Watson, Nancy Dingman, 39, 63
Watts, Mabel, 59
Wise, William, 13, 54, 80
Wynne, Annette, 18

Yolen, Jane, 19
Young, Barbara, 28

Zolotow, Charlotte, 25, 38, 56

ACKNOWLEDGMENTS

Every effort has been made to trace the ownership of all copyrighted material and to secure the necessary permissions to reprint these selections. In the event of any question arising as to the use of any material, the editor and publisher, while expressing regret for any inadvertent error, will be happy to make the necessary correction in future printings.

Grateful acknowledgment is made to the following for permission to reprint and/or record the copyrighted material listed below:

Abingdon Press for "Singing in the Spring" from CHERRY STONES! GARDEN SWINGS! by Ivy O. Eastwick. Copyright © 1962 by Abingdon Press. Used by permission. "Ten to One" and "The Puppy Chased the Sunbeam" from I RODE THE BLACK HORSE FAR AWAY by Ivy O. Eastwick. Copyright © 1960 by Abingdon Press. Used by permission.

Addison-Wesley Publishing Company, Inc., for "Ears Hear" from OODLES OF NOODLES by Lucia M. and James L. Hymes, Jr. Copyright © 1964 by Lucia M. and James L. Hymes, Jr. "Grasshopper Green" and "Makers" from BLUEBERRIES LAVENDER by Nancy Dingman Watson. Copyright © 1977 by Nancy Dingman Watson. Reprinted by permission of Addison-Wesley Publishing Company, Inc.

Atheneum Publishers, Inc., for "Cats and Dogs" from SNOWMAN SNIFFLES by N.M. Bodecker. Copyright © 1983 by N.M. Bodecker. A Margaret K. McElderry Book. "My Dragon" from THE PHANTOM ICE CREAM MAN: MORE NONSENSE POEMS by X.J. Kennedy. Copyright © 1979 by X.J. Kennedy. A Margaret McElderry Book. "Ants Live Here" and "Dragon Smoke" from I FEEL THE SAME WAY. Copyright © 1967 by Lilian Moore. "Bedtime Story" from SOMETHING NEW BEGINS by Lilian Moore. Copyright © 1982 by Lilian Moore. "Night Fun" from IF I WERE IN CHARGE OF THE WORLD by Judith Viorst. Copyright © 1981 by Judith Viorst. Reprinted with the permission of Atheneum Publishers, Inc.

Patricia Ayres for "Toaster Time" from THERE IS NO RHYME FOR SILVER by Eve Merriam. Published by Atheneum Publishers, Inc. Copyright © 1962 by Eve Merriam. Reprinted by permission of the author. All rights reserved.

Kenneth C. Bennett for "When You Talk to a Monkey" and "A Modern Dragon" by Rowena Bennett.

Curtis Brown, Ltd., for "Sneeze" from NO ONE WRITING A LETTER TO A SNAIL by Maxine W. Kumin. Copyright © 1962 by Maxine W. Kumin. "The Swallow" by Ogden Nash from THE NEW NUTCRACKER SUITE AND OTHER INNOCENT VERSES by Ogden Nash. Copyright © 1961, 1962 by Ogden Nash. Reprinted by permission of Curtis Brown, Ltd.

The Caxton Printers Ltd. for "Before the Monkey's Cage" from PICK-POCKET SONGS by Edna Becker. The Caxton Printers Ltd., Caldwell, Idaho. Used by permission.

Laura Cecil for "Run a Little" from THE BLACKBIRD IN THE LILAC by James Reeves. Copyright 1952 by James Reeves. Published by the Oxford University Press. Permission granted by the author's estate.

Marchette Chute for "Drinking Fountain" from AROUND AND ABOUT by Marchette Chute. Copyright © 1957 (E.P. Dutton), renewed 1985. Reprinted by permission of the author.

Lucille Clifton for "April" from EVERETT ANDERSON'S YEAR. Copyright © 1974 by Lucille Clifton. Reprinted by permission of Henry Holt and Company.

William Cole for "Two Sad" by William Cole. Copyright © 1977 by William Cole.

Delacorte Press for "The Toaster" from LAUGHING TIME by William Jay Smith. Copyright © 1953, 1955, 1956, 1957, 1959, 1968, 1974, 1977, 1980 by William Jay Smith. Reprinted by permission of Delacorte Press/Seymour Lawrence. A Merloyd Lawrence Book.

Doubleday & Company, Inc., for "Picnic Day" from A LITTLE BOX OF DAYS by Rachel Field. Copyright 1927 by Doubleday & Company, Inc. "I'd Like to Be a Lighthouse" from TAXIS AND TOADSTOOLS by Rachel Field. Copyright 1926 by Doubleday & Company, Inc. "December" from GAY GO UP by Rose Fyleman. Copyright 1929, 1930 by Doubleday & Company, Inc. Reprinted by permission of the publisher. Canadian rights administered by The Society of Authors.

E.P. Dutton, Inc., for "Icy" and "Under the Ground" from STORIES TO BEGIN ON by Rhoda W. Bacmeister. Copyright 1940 by E.P. Dutton, Inc., renewed 1968 by Rhoda W. Bacmeister. "Jump or Jiggle" by Evelyn Beyer from ANOTHER HERE AND NOW STORYBOOK by Lucy Sprague Mitchell. Copyright 1937 by E.P. Dutton, Inc., renewed 1965 by Lucy Sprague Mitchell. "Crayons," "My Teddy Bear," "Showers," and "Sleeping Outdoors" from RHYMES ABOUT US by Marchette Chute, Copyright © 1974 by Marchette Chute, "Woodpecker in Disguise" from BIRD IN THE BUSH by Grace Taber Hallock. Copyright 1930 by E.P. Dutton, Inc., renewed 1958 by Grace Taber Hallock. "The More It Snows" from THE HOUSE AT POOH CORNER by A.A. Milne, Copyright 1928 by E.P. Dutton, Inc., renewed 1956 by A.A. Milne. "Halfway Down" from WHEN WE WERE VERY YOUNG by A.A. Milne, Copyright 1924 by E.P. Dutton, Inc., renewed 1952 by A.A. Milne. Canadian rights administered by McClellan and Stewart Limited, Toronto. "The Snail and the Mouse" from I HAVE A SONG TO SING TO YOU by Laura E. Richards. Copyright 1938 by D. Appleton-Century Co., Inc. A Hawthorn Book. Reprinted by permission of E.P. Dutton, Inc., a division of New American Library.

Aileen Fisher for "Open House," "Pussy Willows," and "Snail's Pace" from IN THE WOODS, IN THE MEADOW, IN THE SKY by Aileen Fisher. Charles Scribner's Sons, 1965. By permission of the author.

Harcourt Brace Jovanovich, Inc., for "We Built a Castle Near the Rocks" from MORNING IS A LITTLE CHILD by Joan Walsh Anglund.

Harper & Row, Publishers, Inc., for "First Snow," "Five Years Old," and "The Mitten Song" from A POCKETFUL OF POEMS by Marie Louise Allen. Copyright 1939 by Harper & Row, Publishers, Inc., renewed 1956 by Merle Marston Garthwaite. "Keziah" and "Robert, Who Is Often a Stranger to Himself" from BRONZEVILLE BOYS AND GIRLS by Gwendolyn Brooks. Copyright © 1956 by Gwendolyn Brooks Blakely. "Someone's Face" from THE MAN WHO SANG THE SILLIES by John Ciardi (J.B. Lippincott Co.). Copyright © 1961 by John Ciardi. "Wouldn't You?" from YOU READ TO ME, I'LL READ TO YOU by John Ciardi (J.B. Lippincott Co.). Copyright © 1961 by John Ciardi. "Bedtime" and "Moon-Come-Out" from ELEANOR FARJEON'S POEMS FOR CHILDREN (J.B. Lippincott Co.) by Eleanor Farjeon. "Fairies" from ELEANOR FARJEON'S POEMS FOR CHILDREN (J.B. Lippincott Co.) by Eleanor Farjeon. Copyright 1926, 1954 by Eleanor Farjeon. "But I Wonder . . ." from OUT IN THE DARK AND DAYLIGHT: POEMS BY AILEEN FISHER. Copyright © 1980 by Aileen Fisher. "Raindrops" from OUT IN THE DARK AND DAYLIGHT: POEMS BY AILEEN FISHER. Copyright © 1966 by Aileen Fisher. "At Night" from OUT IN THE DARK AND DAYLIGHT: POEMS BY AILEEN FISHER. Copyright © 1973 by Aileen Fisher. "Wings" and "On Halloween" from OUT IN THE DARK AND DAYLIGHT: POEMS BY AILEEN FISHER. Copyright © 1980 by Aileen Fisher. "Peter and Wendy" from BREAD AN' JAM by Wymond Garthwaite. Copyright 1928 by Harper

& Row, Publishers, Inc., renewed 1956 by Merle Marston Garthwaite. "Happy Winter, Steamy Tub" from HAPPY WINTER by Karen Gundersheimer. Copyright © 1982 by Karen Gundersheimer. "Giraffes Don't Huff" from ROAR AND MORE by Karla Kuskin. Copyright © 1956 by Karla Kuskin. "Snow" and "The Gold-Tinted Dragon" from DOGS AND DRAGONS, TREES AND DREAMS: A COLLECTION OF POEMS BY KARLA KUSKIN. Copyright © 1958 by Karla Kuskin. "The Meal" from DOGS AND DRAGONS, TREES AND DREAMS: A COLLECTION OF POEMS BY KARLA KUSKIN. Copyright © 1962 by Karla Kuskin. "There Was a Small Pig Who Wept Tears" from THE BOOK OF PIGERICKS by Arnold Lobel. Copyright © 1983 by Arnold Lobel. "Little Seeds" from THE WINDS THAT COME FROM FAR AWAY AND OTHER POEMS by Else Holmelund Minarik. Copyright © 1964 by Else Holmelund Minarik. "A Frog and a Flea" from HALLOWEEN HECATE AND OTHER RHYMES TO SKIP TO by Cynthia Mitchell (Thomas Y. Crowell Co.). Copyright © 1978 by Cynthia Mitchell. "January" from CHICKEN SOUP WITH RICE: A BOOK OF MONTHS by Maurice Sendak. Copyright © 1962 by Maurice Sendak. "Ducks in the Rain" from CRICKETY CRICKET! THE BEST-LOVED POEMS OF JAMES S. TIPPETT. Copyright © 1973 by Martha K. Tippett. "Belly & Tubs Went Out in a Boat" from FATHER FOX'S PENNYRHYMES by Clyde Watson (Thomas Y. Crowell Co.). Text copyright © 1971 by Clyde Watson. "The House Cat" from FOR DAYS AND DAYS by Annette Wynne (J.B. Lippincott Co.). Copyright 1919 by Harper & Row, Publishers, Inc., renewed 1947 by Annette Wynne. "The Top and the Tip" and "Look" from ALL THAT SUNLIGHT: POEMS BY CHARLOTTE ZOLOTOW. Copyright © 1967 by Charlotte Zolotow. "The Spring Wind" from RIVER WINDING: POEMS BY CHARLOTTE ZOLOTOW (Thomas Y. Crowell Co.). Copyright © 1970 by Charlotte Zolotow.

Margaret Hillert for "Hide-and-Seek Shadow," "My Teddy Bear," and "Blowing Bubbles" from FARTHER THAN FAR. Copyright © 1969 by Follett Publishing Co. Used by permission of the author, who controls all rights.

Houghton Mifflin Company for "if I Were Bigger Than Anyone" from WONDER WHY by Ruth Harnden. Copyright © 1971 by Ruth Harnden, "Night Comes" from A BUNCH OF POEMS AND VERSES by Beatrice Schenk de Regniers. Copyright © 1977 by Beatrice Schenk de Regniers. Reprinted by permission of Houghton Mifflin Company.

Ruth W. Jackson for "How a Puppy Grows" and "Fun" from THE JOLLY JUNGLE PICTURE BOOK by Leroy F. Jackson. Rand McNally, 1926.

Barbara Boyden Jordan for "Mud" by Polly Chase Boyden.

May Justus for "Good Neighbors" by May Justus from MICE ARE RATHER NICE, compiled by Vardine Moore, Atheneum, 1981.

Bobbi Katz for "Cat Kisses," copyright © 1974, "Unfortunately," copyright © 1976, and "Pretending," copyright © 1973.

Lerner Publications Co. for "Umbrellas" from SWING AROUND THE SUN by Barbara Juster Esbensen. Copyright © 1965 by Lerner Publications Co. Used by permission of the publisher.

The Literary Trustees of Walter de la Mare and the Society of Authors as their representative for "The Huntsmen" and "Here All We See" by Walter de la Mare.

Little, Brown and Company for "Snowman" from ONE AT A TIME by David McCord. Copyright © 1974 by David McCord.

Marci Ridlon McGill for "Hamsters" and "Johnny" from THAT WAS SUMMER by Marci Ridlon. Copyright © 1969 by Marci Ridlon. Published by Follett Publishing Co.

McGraw-Hill Book Company for "Squirrel in the Rain" from THE LITTLE WHISTLER by Frances Frost and "Fuzzy Wuzzy, Creepy Crawly" from HEY BUG! by Lillian Schulz.

Gail Kredenser Mack for "Polar Bear" from THE ABC OF BUMPTIOUS BEASTS by Gail Kredenser. Copyright © 1966 by Gail Kredenser. Published by Harlin Quist.

David McKay Co., Inc., for "The World" from CHRISTOPHER O! by Barbara Young. Copyright 1947. Reprinted by permission of David McKay Co., Inc.

Macmillan of Canada, a Division of Canada Publishing Corp., for "Skyscraper" from ALLIGATOR PIE by Dennis Lee. "The Dreadful Doings of Jelly Belly," "Good Night, Good Night," "Silverly," and "Three Tickles" from JELLY BELLY by Dennis Lee. Reprinted by permission of Macmillan of Canada, a Division of Canada Publishing Corp.

Macmillan Publishing Co., Inc., for "The Toad" from SUMMER GREEN by Elizabeth Coatsworth. Copyright 1948 by Macmillan Publishing Co., Inc., renewed 1976 by Elizabeth Coatsworth Beston. "The Little Turtle" from COLLECTED POEMS by Vachel Lindsay. Copyright 1920 by Macmillan Publishing Co., Inc., renewed 1948 by Elizabeth C. Lindsay. "An Explanation of the Grasshopper" and "The Moon's the North Wind's Cooky" from COLLECTED POEMS by Vachel Lindsay. Copyright 1914 by Macmillan Publishing Co., Inc., renewed 1942 by Elizabeth C. Lindsay. "Mix a Pancake" from SING-SONG by Christina G. Rossetti (New York: Macmillan, 1924).

Methuen, Inc., for "Mother Cat's Purr" from DRAGON NIGHT AND OTHER LULLABIES by Jane Yolen. Copyright © 1980 by Jane Yolen. Published by Methuen, Inc., 733 Third Avenue, New York, NY 10017.

James N. Miller for "Shore" by Mary Britton Miller.

Spike Milligan Productions Ltd. for "My Sister Laura" and "Tell Me Little Woodworm" from SILLY VERSE FOR KIDS by Spike Milligan.

William Morrow & Company, Inc., for "Covers" from VACATION TIME by Nikki Giovanni. Copyright © 1980 by Nikki Giovanni. By permission of William Morrow & Company, Inc. "Home" from EVERYBODY HAS TWO EYES by Jean Jaszi (Lothrop, Lee & Shepard Books, 1956). "It Fell in the City" and "Five Little Monsters" from BLACKBERRY INK by Eve Merriam. Copyright © 1985 by Eve Merriam. By permission of William Morrow & Company, Inc. "Moon Boat" from ALL ASLEEP by Charlotte Pomerantz. Copyright © 1984 by Charlotte Pomerantz. By permission of Greenwillow Books (A Division of William Morrow & Company, Inc.). "The Mistletoe" from IT'S CHRISTMAS by Jack Prelutsky. Copyright © 1981 by Jack Prelutsky. "Skeleton Parade" from IT'S HALLOWEEN by Jack Prelutsky. Copyright © 1977 by Jack Prelutsky. "Sometimes," "Somersaults," and "Whistling" from RAINY RAINY SATURDAY by Jack Prelutsky. Copyright © 1980 by Jack Prelutsky. "The House Mouse" from ZOO DOINGS by Jack Prelutsky. Copyright © 1974, 1983 by Jack Prelutsky. By permission of Greenwillow Books (A Division of William Morrow & Company, Inc.).

The Nature Conservancy for "Dragonfly" by Florence Page Jaques. Reprinted by permission of the Nature Conservancy.

Penguin Books Ltd. for "It's Eleven O'Clock" from STICKLEBACK, STICKLEBACK by Nancy Chambers (Kestrel Books, 1977). Copyright © 1977 by Nancy Chambers. Reprinted by permission of Penguin Books Ltd.

Anita E. Posey for "When All the World's Asleep" by Anita E. Posey.

The Putnam Publishing Group for "Big," "Dangerous," "Naughty Soap Song," and "The Picnic" from ALL TOGETHER by Dorothy Aldis, copyright 1925–1928, 1934, 1939, 1952, renewed 1953–1956, 1962, 1967 by Dorothy Aldis. Reprinted by permission of G.P. Putnam's Sons. "Crunch and Lick" from IS ANYBODY HUNGRY? by Dorothy Aldis. Copyright © 1964 by Dorothy Aldis. Reprinted by permission of G.P. Putnam's Sons. "Sun After Rain" from SMALL WONDERS by Norma Farber. Copyright © 1964, 1968, 1969 by Norma Farber. Reprinted by permission of Coward, McCann, & Geoghegan. "Hushabye My Darling" from CATCH ME AND KISS ME AND SAY IT AGAIN by Clyde Watson. Reprinted by permission of Philomel Books.

Rand McNally & Co. for "I Can Be a Tiger" by Mildred Leigh Anderson, from *Child Life Magazine*. Copyright 1924, 1952 by Rand McNally & Co. "The Butterfly" by Clinton Scollard from *Child Life Magazine*. Copyright 1924, 1952 by Rand McNally & Co.

Random House, Inc., for "Ode to Spring" from THE COLLECTED POEMS OF FREDDY THE PIG by Walter R. Brooks. Copyright 1953 by Walter R. Brooks. Reprinted by permission of Alfred A. Knopf, Inc. "Winter Sweetness" from THE DREAM KEEPER AND OTHER POEMS by Langston Hughes. Copyright 1932 and renewed 1960 by Langston Hughes. Reprinted by permission of Alfred A. Knopf, Inc. "Quack! Quack!" from OH SAY CAN YOU SAY? by Dr. Seuss. Copyright © 1979 by Dr. Seuss and A.S. Geisel. Reprinted by permission of Random House, Inc.

Marian Reiner for "Just Watch" from WHISPERS AND OTHER POEMS by Myra Cohn Livingston. Copyright © 1958 by Myra Cohn Livingston. "Wide Awake" from WIDE AWAKE AND OTHER POEMS by Myra Cohn Livingston. Copyright © 1959 by Myra Cohn Livingston. Reprinted by permission of Marian Reiner for the author.

David Ross for "Good-Morning" by Muriel Sipe.

Louise H. Sclove for "Chums" by Arthur Guiterman. Reprinted by permission of Louise H. Sclove.

Norah Smaridge for "Footnote" and "Toothsome." Reprinted by permission of the author.

Karen S. Solomon for "Poor Shadow" from I WATCH THE WORLD GO BY by Ilo Orleans. "The Frog on the Log" from THE ZOO THAT GREW by Ilo Orleans. Reprinted by permission of Karen S. Solomon.

Arnold Spilka for "Slippery Sam" from A RUMBUDGIN OF NONSENSE by Arnold Spilka. Copyright © 1970 by Arnold Spilka.

Dorothy Brown Thompson for "Wish." Copyright 1944. Reprinted by permission of the author.

Union of American Hebrew Congregations for "Dreidel Song" by Efraim Rosenzweig.

Viking Penguin, Inc., for "In the Summer We Eat" from BITS AND PIECES by Zhenya Gay. "Ants," "Fish," and "Yellow Butter" from YELLOW BUTTER PURPLE JELLY RED JAM BLACK BREAD by Mary Ann Hoberman. Copyright © 1981 by Mary Ann Hoberman. "Birthdays" and "Firefly" from UNDER THE TREE by Elizabeth Madox Roberts. Copyright 1922 by B.W. Heubsch, Inc. Copyright renewed 1950 by Ivor S. Roberts. "Joyful" from FROM SUMMER TO SUMMER by Rose Burgunder Styron. Copyright © 1965 by Rose Styron. Reprinted by permission of Viking Penguin, Inc.

Mabel Watts for "Yesterday's Paper." Reprinted by permission of Mabel Watts.

William Wise for "Just Three," "Rainy Day," and "Runaway" from ALL ON A SUMMER DAY. Copyright © 1971 by William Wise. Reprinted by permission of William Wise.